The Lost Hero

Kathy Wall

ISBN-13: 9781723734250

Chapter 1

Sandra Wilkins escorted her Aunt Molly toward a bench near the check-out lanes at the Soriana. She looked around at a peaceful scene. Few people were in the store, and two cashiers chatted. Everything seemed so calm, how could anything go wrong?

Her aunt was in pain and needed to get home. Would she be safe sitting alone? Sandra had heard about muggings and robberies in this part of the world. If she hurried, maybe everything would be okay. One thing's for sure, Auntie M wasn't going anywhere soon.

"You wait here. I'll take care of the groceries."

"Sorry to flake out on you. Sometimes I just run out of energy." Auntie M sank onto the bench. She put her purse in her lap and wrapped her arms around it. Her left arm supported the right one in the sling. She sighed.

"It's no problem." *At least I hope it's not.* "You just rest for a few minutes."

"Thank you."

Sandra smiled as she rushed back to her cart. She headed to the first open check-out register. Fear mounted in her throat as she turned into the lane.

How difficult can this be? She emptied the few items in her cart onto the conveyer belt.

"*¿Encontraste todo lo que buscabas?*"

Hopefully, the woman had asked if everything was okay. Sandra nodded.

The clerk scanned the seven items.

Sandra took a deep breath. She could do this. Aunt Molly's eyes were closed. She was slumped in relaxation, and her chest had the rhythmic rise and fall of sleep. This would be over soon. Then she would drive them back to her aunt's house.

"*Será 683 pesos.*"

Sandra handed the woman her credit card.

She swiped it through the machine on top of her register. The contraption beeped. "*Lo siento, señorita, aceptamos esta marca de tarjeta.* " She handed the card back to her.

With a sigh, Sandra stepped toward the bags of groceries at the end of the counter. Whew, that wasn't so bad.

"*Disculpe, señora. Eso será 683 pesos.*"

Sandra tipped her head slightly, trying to figure out what the clerk had said. She handed her credit card back to the woman.

"*¿Tiene otra forma de pago?*"

Sandra stared at the clerk. *What's wrong? What does she want?*

The woman at the end of the counter moved her two bags of groceries away from the aisle. Like she

2

was protecting them from being stolen.

"I'm sorry. I don't understand." They probably didn't comprehend English any more than she understood Spanish. Her stomach churned violently.

"¿No tendra's efectivo? Porque necesito recibir tu pago."

What would these women do if she walked over to the bench and woke up Aunt Molly? Would they scream at her?

She started for the bench. The hefty woman who had bagged her groceries blocked the exit.

Sandra pointed to her aunt. "I need to wake her up, so she can give me the money you need or at least help me understand what's happening."

The large woman didn't move.

Now what? She had over $100 in US currency in her purse. She also had two other credit cards but hadn't activated them for use in Mexico. She had a handful of one-peso coins in her pocket.

"Do you take American money?"

The middle-aged woman at the register didn't say anything. A frown inched its way across her face.

Sandra didn't move. She clutched her wallet. Panic rose slowly from the pit in her stomach.

"Do you need some help?" A warm, rich baritone voice behind her spoke in unaccented American English.

"Yes, I don't know what to do. She won't take my credit card."

She turned to identify the man behind the voice she hoped could solve her problem. Before her stood the most handsome man she had ever seen –

even in the movies. He wasn't much older than she was. His biceps bulged beneath his shirt and exposed a tan line just above the cuff. His skin was the color of honey, and he had curly black hair. His tan accented the laugh lines around his chocolate eyes. *Is he American?*

Tall, dark, good-looking, kind, and compassionate. He was going to solve her money situation. *Unless he's a figment of my imagination?*

Sandra had never understood the term *swoon* before, but she was pretty sure that's what she was feeling right now. Her pulse raced, her breathing slowed, and her mind clogged with the presence of this person.

He spoke to the cashier in beautiful Spanish. It might not have been the right words, but the cashier nodded, so the language was perfect.

He turned to her and smiled. His teeth were pure white and straight. They dazzled enough to create a glow around his head.

She mentally shook herself. *Quit fantasizing and act like a normal human.*

"She said they don't take Discover Cards nor American money. Your bill is 683 pesos."

"The lady napping on the bench is my aunt. I need to rouse her. She has enough money to pay the bill. If not, she has a valid credit card." Sandra was breathless. It took such effort to talk to this magnificent specimen of the human male.

He pulled out his wallet and extracted several bills. "We'll settle up later."

Sandra stared at him. *Who is this person?*

The cashier handed him change. He picked up

the two bags of groceries and escorted her to the bench.

As she walked away from the check-out lane, she handed the bagger two coins.

She stepped beside the snoozing woman. "Aunt Molly." Her voice was just above a whisper.

Her aunt stirred and opened her eyes. "Oh, sweetie. I think I dozed off. Is everything okay?" She shifted her focus to the man beside Sandra.

"Auntie M, I want to introduce…" She stared at the man, then back to her aunt. "My hero."

He stuck out his hand. "I'm Brad Andrews."

When he said his name, the man became real and not the dreamy knight in shining armor she had originally envisioned. He was still handsome, still kind. He became a person she wanted to get to know.

Her aunt stood. "Well, how nice to meet you. So you're a hero?"

"Her opinion only. She thinks I saved her from the jaws of the vicious, domineering cashier." He chuckled.

Sandra stepped beside her aunt. "Well, I want to thank you. I don't think I've ever been so frustrated or fearful as I was before you showed up."

Brad Andrews nodded. He stood there, holding her bags.

"Auntie M, he paid for our groceries, so we need to pay him back. I don't have enough cash, and the store wouldn't take my Discover Card."

"Oh, dear. Mr. Andrews, thank you so much." She opened her purse and removed her wallet. "How much do I owe you?"

"Six hundred eighty-three pesos."

She removed several bills and handed them to Brad. "Keep the change."

He took the money and stuffed it into the pocket of his cargo pants but didn't hand over the groceries.

A warm smile teased the corners of his mouth, and he winked at her aunt. "I'll carry these to your car."

Sandra cradled her aunt's elbow and guided her toward the door. "Now if you'll hand me the keys, I'll drive home."

"No, no, dear. I can drive." The feisty woman stepped off the curb and started across the asphalt at a fast clip.

Not bad for a woman in pain.

Sandra kept pace. "I know you can, but I can too. I drive in Los Angeles regularly. I think I can handle anything Queretaro traffic can throw at me."

Brad followed. He made no comment. How Sandra wished he'd support her in this minor tiff.

As they neared her car, her aunt paused. "Are you sure you're up to this?" Then looking at the handsome man, she giggled. "She's never driven here before. She doesn't understand how aggressive Mexican drivers can be."

"Your arm doesn't need to be driving." Sandra stuck out her hand for the keys.

Aunt Molly rubbed the sling.

"Well, your niece does have a point."

Sandra smiled.

"And your aunt does too."

She frowned. Her hero was turning on her.

"Tell you what. I'll follow you home. Uh, your niece can drive. That way if there's a problem you have another Spanish-speaking person to stand up for you."

"That works for me." Her aunt held up the keys, which Sandra instantly snatched and headed for the driver's door.

She turned to Brad. "That won't be necessary. Just put the groceries in the back, and we'll be on our way." She opened the rear door.

The hero followed directions and set the two bags on the seat. He leaned down and smiled at Molly resting in the passenger seat. He straightened and looked Sandra in the eye. "I'm going to follow you anyway. I told your aunt I would."

"I told you that wasn't necessary." Sandra peppered her words with annoyance. She slammed the back door.

She shivered. Less than a month ago, she broke off her relationship with Joshua because he told her what to do and how to do it. She didn't need another domineering male in her life.

A heart-melting smile spread across his face. "It's important to her." He tipped his head toward Auntie M.

If he was going to be so presumptuous, she'd set him straight. Put him in an awkward position. She could find out just how arrogant this man was. "Well, in that case why don't you stop in for a drink? Uh, for coffee."

"That sounds fun." He grinned.

Sandra's sucked in a deep breath. She didn't think he'd accept. Now what was she going to do?

He walked across the parking lot toward his car. When he reached the black Toyota, he turned toward her. The breeze blew his shirt against his chest revealing rippling muscles.

Sandra got into her Honda CRV. Why was she fighting getting to know this man? He was handsome beyond words and compassionate, intuitive, and outgoing. He would be a great friend, but she was throwing out roadblocks. *Why*? *He's acting like Joshua, that's why*. Was that fair to Brad? To Aunt Molly?

* * *

Brad shook his head as he followed the aunt's car. He could ask why he was going for coffee with this stranger and her aunt. But he knew the answer. She was beautiful, old enough to be a friend, and she was from the US. She spoke English. His ear wanted to hear her talk, his mind wanted to reason with her in his native language.

There was something enigmatic about this woman. He'd heard a unique quality+ in her voice when she didn't know what to do at the store and seen it in her eyes. He couldn't call it confidence, but it was something he'd never encountered.

For several months, he'd been homesick for America, but he had another eight to ten weeks on this project before he could return to the States. His heart yearned to converse and to laugh and joke in English.

He'd even thought about flying home to St. Louis for a weekend. But he wasn't sure he could take the questions and fears his family always presented. His mom thought he lived in the middle of a cartel camp with his life in jeopardy every second. He told her this was the safest city in Mexico, but that didn't ease her fears.

At one point about a month ago, he'd considered going to LA and taking a tour of Hollywood just to be with Americans. But the prospect of eating alone nixed the plan. He could do that here. Besides, probably the only ones taking the tours were Japanese.

The stranger turned into a gated community, and he followed. Her driving was perfect. He'd feared she'd be too slow for the Mexican streets, but she did fine. He was pretty sure she'd pulled in front of several cars as she raced down the Cinco de Febrero hoping to lose him in traffic. He didn't have an address for her destination, so if he lost her, she'd be gone forever. Her tactics were typical of Mexican driving, so he stayed right with her.

When she pulled into a carport, he parked along the curb. Aunt Molly hopped out of the car and waved at him. She bore a huge grin.

The younger woman retrieved the groceries. As she walked around the back of the car the sun struck her blonde hair making it look like spun gold. *Why didn't I notice that earlier?* Her robin's egg blue eyes seemed to welcome him, unlike the chill before. If he played his cards right, he wouldn't have to eat alone tonight.

Now all he had to do was find out who she was.

* * *

All the way home, Sandra had to listen to Aunt Molly bestow praises about such a nice young man. She'd tried to lose him in the heavy traffic on the highway, but he'd managed to stay right with her.

Somewhere along the trip, she stopped fighting her desire to shrug him off. Brad made Aunt Molly happy for some reason. Maybe she liked harmlessly flirting with a younger man. Whatever it was, her favorite aunt exhibited a spunk Sandra hadn't seen since she arrived last week. She'd do whatever it took to see that joy continue.

She pulled into the carport, grabbed the groceries from the back seat, and headed toward the house. Brad joined them on the sidewalk. Her best role would be innocent damsel. "I was afraid I'd lost you on the highway a couple of times."

He chuckled.

He knows what I was doing. Her face burned.

"You fit right in. It's like you've been driving here for years." He stepped forward and opened the door Aunt Molly unlocked.

Sandra headed for the large kitchen to the left. "How do you like your coffee?"

"Actually, I really don't need any coffee right now." He escorted Aunt Molly to her recliner. "I have a confession to make. I heard you at the store and wanted to talk."

Sandra came around the corner into the living room. "Talk?"

"Exactly." He sat in the chair next to her aunt. "I've been working here for just over a year now. My Spanish has gotten quite good, and I use it almost exclusively. But when I heard your American accent today, I was overwhelmed with homesickness. I just wanted to talk to someone in English. Does that even make sense?"

"It does to me." Aunt Molly pushed the button releasing the leg support of the chair. "I've been here less than six months, and I sometimes go to the clubhouse just to visit with other Americans."

Embarrassed, Sandra ducked back into the kitchen. She'd misinterpreted the man's motives. He wasn't an arrogant playboy, but a lonely English-speaking soul in need of fellowship. A very handsome one at that. Way out of her league.

And she hadn't even introduced herself.

Chapter 2

Sandra retrieved the plastic container of homemade chocolate chip cookies from the shelf and arranged the treats on a plate. She smiled. She'd made these for Aunt Molly a few days ago to ward off Auntie's melancholy. They worked magic on her, maybe they would on him. Homesickness is no fun.

The coffee finished brewing. She poured three cups and set them on the tray with the cookies, napkins, creamer, and sugar. As she carried the treats into the living room, she sensed she would have made a perfect 1950's hostess. She almost giggled.

"What do you do here?" Sandy looked deep into Brad's brown eyes. The emptiness she saw surprised her.

"I'm a construction manager." He picked up the plate and held it toward Aunt Molly.

"And what do you construct?" Her aunt chose a

small cookie near the edge.

"Currently, I'm in charge of a building at Arkansas State University." He sat the plate on the tray and chose the largest cookie from the center.

"Arkansas State? In Mexico?" Sandra gasped as she reached for a cup of coffee.

"It's a new project." He stared into his cup.

"Seriously, an American university in Queretaro?" She bit into her cookie.

"Construction on the campus started two years ago. Just over a year ago, the buildings began. To date, we have six structures completed. Two dorms, three classroom buildings and an administration complex. Classes will start this summer." He relaxed in his chair.

"You managed all that?" *Aren't you a little young to be in charge of such a major project?* Sandra sipped her coffee.

"I'm in charge of the science building. We're having a bit of trouble getting equipment delivered. I spend most of my time on the phone talking to suppliers. Things work a little differently here in Mexico."

Aunt Molly reached for a second cookie. "That's pretty impressive."

"It's part of my doctorate program." He seemed to delight in offering tiny bits of information one speck at a time.

Her aunt shook her head. "Your what?"

"I'm getting my PhD in international construction engineering. I still have my dissertation to write, but the science building is my research project. I'm specializing in building using

American standards in countries outside the US." From the tone of his voice, he could have been discussing the value of kale to your diet.

Sandra's ears burned. She'd thought he'd been bragging. That's twice she'd misjudged the man.

"What happened to your arm?" His focus was on Aunt Molly.

"I fell going down some steps at a friend's house. Broke both bones in my forearm." She raised the sling into the air as if that explained everything.

"Is it in a cast? I've only seen the tips of your fingers." He sipped his coffee.

"Until a week from Monday. But it still hurts." Auntie M put her empty cup on the tray and leaned back in her chair. "That's why Sandra's here. I've been having trouble getting about and doing things, so she came to help until I'm healed. She's been an angel."

Brad turned to Sandra.

"So, it's Sandra? She's an angel?" A smile ripped across his face.

"Indeed she is. I don't think I could have managed without her. She's been a great help, and she speaks English." Her teasing tone wasn't lost on her listeners.

"I'm on vacation." Sandra felt her face heating.

"From what?" Brad set his cup on the tray.

"I graduated from UCLA in December. Teaching jobs are a bit difficult to find this time of year. I've been substituting, which I do not like." *And Joshua would not leave me alone.* Since graduation when she told him she didn't think their relationship could go anywhere and they should call it quits, he'd been increasingly possessive. "So when Auntie M called, I jumped at the chance to explore a new country and culture before my meager savings ran out." She stood and picked up the tray.

"I haven't been a very good hostess. We haven't gone anywhere or done anything. I'm afraid her experience in Mexico has been sitting around the house with an old woman who's trying to heal from a badly broken arm. Not much exploring going on here." Her aunt sounded tired.

"That's not true. Everything has been such an adventure. Like today's trip to the mall and the grocery store. I don't know what I was expecting, but both those places could have been dropped into any town in American without any problems, except for the Spanish, of course. No culture shock here. I think I was expecting dirt floors and to see chickens running around the grocery store." Sandra laughed as she headed toward the kitchen.

She heard Auntie M yawn.

"Well, since you haven't been exploring, why don't I take you ladies to the city center tomorrow? We can do some shopping and have lunch. It's a fun place to explore." He stood.

"Oh, that sounds delightful." Auntie M scooted to the front of her chair. "What time?"

"Ten, ten-thirty?" His eyes never left her aunt.

"Sounds great. You driving?" Aunt Molly started to stand. Brad stepped to her side and offered his assistance.

"I certainly am. I even know where to park." He chuckled.

"Sandra. We're going to the city center tomorrow." She finally glanced in her niece's direction. "Is that okay with you?"

She couldn't say no. Not with her aunt so excited. "Sounds fun." *Not even going to ask if you're up to it.* The outing today had worn her aunt out. Could she even handle an excursion tomorrow? One day at a time.

"We're all set then." The warm baritone voice that saved her at the check-out lane sent tingles down Sandra's spine.

* * *

Saturday dawned bright and sunny. The brightness matched Sandra's excitement. She used the curling iron to puff up her hair for the first time since arriving and pulled her dress black slacks from the closet. Nope, too dressy. She chose a pair of khaki shorts and a dark blue tank top. She topped the outfit with a brown and blue plaid linen shirt. Yelp, very classic. No one will be embarrassed by this American tourist. Blue flats finished her outfit. Putting on make-up took twice as long as normal. She'd be ready for that handsome man who would show up at their door in two hours.

Sounds and smells of breakfast announced Aunt Molly was up. She hurried down the steps.

"I smelled the bacon." Sandra smiled as she entered the kitchen.

"I made breakfast." Her aunt greeted her from the kitchen as she stepped into the living room. Her aunt was as excited as she was yesterday. *That's a good sign.*

"I hope Mr. Brad comes at ten. I know that's

early for the shops to open, but I'm so thrilled to go downtown." Her aunt walked to the table carrying two plates, each full of bacon, scramble eggs and toast. One was balanced on her cast and held in place by her thumb.

"Haven't you ever been?" *What a silly question. She's a history/culture buff and has lived here six months.* Surely, she'd been downtown.

"Nope. No one ever wanted to go, and I don't like going by myself." Auntie M put the plates of food down. She rubbed her sling as she sat.

"Not even your friend Ellen?" Sandra walked to the refrigerator for apple butter and orange juice. She picked up two glasses as she returned to the table.

Auntie M's smile vanished, and she stilled. Sadness descended on her like a thick dark cloud. "Ellen and I have been friends since college. I thought we had so much in common." She poked her eggs. With a sigh, she scooped a forkful of the fluffy yellow concoction. "I was wrong."

"I'm so sorry." If her aunt's friend wasn't that close, what was Aunt Molly doing here? She'd come down with Ellen to enjoy their retirement years.

"Me, too. I should have known. I'm not even sure she's a Christian. I invited her to a Bible study and she refused to come. Gave me every excuse in the book. That should have been a clue something was amiss."

"What about your other friends?"

The woman lowered her fork and rested her chin on the fist of her good arm. "I don't really have any friends here. Just a bunch of acquaintances. I don't like going bar hopping, drinking or partying, so I don't really fit in. Haven't found anyone who quilts either. So, I pretty much manage alone."

"Oh, Auntie M, that's terrible. Why do you stay?" Sandra sipped her orange juice.

The older woman shrugged. "The lease is up in four months. It's just easier to stay put until then."

"Well, today we're going exploring. Are you sure you're up to this?"

"Sweetie, I wouldn't miss this for the world." She resumed her egg eating with gusto.

Brad arrived at ten minutes after ten. Aunt Molly had been pacing the floor since nine-thirty.

When she saw him, Sandra rushed to the door and jerked it open. "I'm so happy to see you."

He grinned. "Delighted to hear *that*."

She swatted his arm. "Aunt Molly is *so* ready to go. You're on track to becoming her favorite hero. Seems no one wanted to go sightseeing with her, until you came along."

"Just a bunch of old fuddy-duddies living around here. They need some new blood." Her aunt walked toward the door with her purse slung over her arm. "Are we ready to go? Sandra, get your bag." Auntie M headed out the door toward Brad's car.

Her aunt reached for the backdoor latch.

"No, Auntie M. You sit in the front seat. You can see better." Sandra held open the door.

Her aunt glanced across the hood to Brad who nodded and winked. A huge grin spread across her aunt's face, and she slid into the car. Carefully she placed her sling on top of her purse.

They took the Febrero for what seemed forever. Brad pointed out different sights to which her aunt oohed and ahhed. Cars whizzed by within inches, but Brad hardly noticed.

Sandra was amazed how much this looked like American cities. Although most of the building signs were in Spanish, there were enough taco shops, Subways, and Kentucky Fried Chicken stores to make it appear normal. The highway didn't have a shoulder, and an access road ran right beside the main highway. Only a curb separated the two lanes.

They turned off the Fabrero onto another main street with traffic signals. Ahead the remains of an ancient stone viaduct dominated their view. The structure four or five stories tall once supplied water to the town.

Auntie M took photos through the windshield.

Brad wove through the narrow streets with ease. He moved into the left lane and descended into an underground parking garage.

At the bottom of the ramp, he stopped beside a flight of concrete steps. "I'm going to let you out here. Walk to the top of the steps and wait for me near the newspaper stand."

Sandra and Molly exited and followed directions. The walked up the steep steps past a couple of young kids selling trinkets. Sandra proceeded slowly beside her aunt who clung to the handrail and stepped onto each riser with one foot then brought the other to the same step. She paused every four or five steps to draw a deep breath.

I hope we can find a seat for Auntie M once we

get to the top.

They stepped out of the dark pit into a beautiful plaza. Huge paving stones covered an entire city block. Sculptures, a fountain, unique boxed streetlights, and benches were scattered about the large space.

The plaza was spotless. Hunchbacked ladies strolled around with brooms made from branches. Trees with carefully trimmed canopies ran along all sides providing shade and noise barriers.

Through their branches, Sandra could see the surrounding buildings had arches on the first floor. Most stores were painted in the umbers, deep yellows, and brick reds she expected to find in Mexico. This definitely was not the USA.

The sweet scents of blossoming flowers tickled her nose. Perhaps that was jasmine, the only flower Sandra knew that gave off inviting smells. She'd have to ask Brad about that when he joined them.

Aunt Molly grabbed her arm. "This is what I came to see." Her voice cracked with emotion.

Her aunt twirled around, soaking in the scene before her like a country girl landing in Times Square for the first time.

"So, what do you think?" Brad stepped beside her aunt.

"It's beautiful, simply beautiful. Thank you for bringing me."

"There's more to explore. Ready?" He extended his elbow for Aunt Molly to grasp.

"Ready." She grabbed the crook of his arm.

Brad grinned when he glanced at Sandra. He nodded and winked.

"Me, too." She slipped her arm around her aunt's waist, carefully avoiding the sling.

They walked down the wide sidewalk while cars rumbled along the cobblestoned street. At the corner, they turned left and headed up a gently sloping walkway. The area was wide enough for one car or several dozen tourists. No cars allowed.

In the center of the converted lane, kiosks owners rolled plastic tarps up onto a rack near the roofline of their small wooden stalls. Open for business. Displays of scarves, dresses and ribbon headbands decorated the town shopping center designed especially for tourists. The shopkeepers yelled greetings to one another. Echoes of the salutations blended with mariachi music and bounced off the ancient buildings sounding like thousands at a football game.

About every fifty yards they'd pass a woman in typical tribal garb selling handmade Otomi dolls. Some of the women were sitting, working on another doll. Others walked about with small children tugging on their skirts carrying trays displaying their wares.

Sandra felt she had stepped into another world. The language, dress, and colors brought a sense of timeliness. She and Aunt Molly took pictures with their phones. There's no way she could describe all that she saw without a photo to show.

They walked beside a two-story wall painted a rich brick red surrounded by a wrought iron fence. Inside the wall, Sandra saw a church. The support wall of the dome was painted a deep yellow, almost ochre. A tiled curved roof glittered in the sunlight led to a cupola topped with a massive cross. The gates were open into the courtyard filled with trees and flowers.

"Can we go in?" Sandra stepped toward the opening.

"Not today. They're having mass." Brad pointed to a sign. "Most churches in Queretaro don't welcome visitors wandering around inside."

"I thought they liked to show off their beautiful interiors." Aunt Molly watched a couple hurry past.

Brad chuckled. "Most churches here don't have beautiful interiors, just functional altars and stuff."

The small group continued to the adjacent plaza with a statue of a dancing Aztec Indian with a fancy headdress.

"If you want to see the elaborate interior of a church we'll go to Guanajuato. There's a cathedral there that will knock your socks off."

"That sounds fun." Aunt Molly skipped a few steps forward. She looked like a marionette with her black sling bobbing in front of her as she swayed her hips. "I'm so glad Sandra ran out of money at the store and you rescued her. You also rescued me."

Sandra's face burned. She didn't run out of money. She just didn't have the right stuff. But Auntie M's joy was overflowing, and Sandra had no intention of slowing it down. "Sounds like that town is on our list of things to do."

"No problem. It's a two-hour drive, and an all-day trip. We'll put it on the schedule."

Sandra's heart quickened. Today wasn't a one-time deal. He planned to be their guide in the future.

She knew Aunt Molly would be happy, but she was surprised how pleased she was.

As they walked along, Brad pointed out small carvings of Inca heroes on the cornerstones of many buildings. Sandra would have missed them if he hadn't been here.

They strolled past small shops tucked behind arched doorways. Some stores weren't much wider than their doorways. You could almost touch both walls if you extended your arms.

"It's about lunch-time. Ready for a sit-down break?"

Sandra nodded, but wasn't thrilled at the thought of ordering from a Spanish menu. She certainly didn't want to end up with something raw or slimy.

But Brad was here. All would be well.

Chapter 3

Sandra's concern grew as they neared a row of restaurants. She was the only one who couldn't read Spanish.

Brad stepped closer. "They have English menus."

Sandra breathed a sigh of relief. "Good."

"And American-style food. So, if you order a steak here, you'll get a regular grilled steak. And their mashed potatoes are mashed potatoes." He led the way across the plaza to a restaurant with a wrought iron fence marking off the outdoor eating area. An overhead awning protected them from the sun.

Evidently this was a place Brad liked to come for his American food fix. The waiters greeted him with wide grins.

After turning down the grasshopper soup, Sandra repeated Brad's order for steak with mashed potatoes. Aunt Molly went for the salmon. They ordered in English. Brad promptly repeated their requests in Spanish.

A basket of thick tortilla chips, a dish of peppers in a clear marinade, and a bowl of a yellowish-tan spread were artfully arranged on the table.

Aunt Molly stuck her fork into a pepper and started to take a bite.

"Start small, those tend to be pretty hot," Brad warned.

She nodded and took a nibble off the small globe. She dropped her fork to the plate and reached for her glass of water with her good hand and the fingers protruding from the cast.

"Yes," She coughed. "Hot."

They all laughed. The waiter hurried over to refill her glass.

"You might like the spread. It's a cross between cheese and hummus. A house specialty." He dipped his knife into the creamy mixture and smeared it across a chip. When he bit down the chip crumbled, and he caught the pieces in his hand.

Sandra broke her chip before adding the tan concoction. She popped it into her mouth. "That's good!"

Aunt Molly dipped her chip into the bowl and crunched. "Yum."

Before they emptied the container, their meals were delivered. Three waiters walked behind the table with sizzling plates in hand. In unison, they put the plates on the table all in keeping with the background music.

"If it's your order and it's appealing, look at the server and nod." Brad's voice was barely above a whisper.

As the men stepped away from the table, Auntie M put her hands together even though one was deeply buried in the sling. "If you don't mind, I'll pray for our food."

The request evidently surprised Brad. He looked like cold water had been thrown in his face. The English-speaking man needed more than fellowship.

Aunt Molly ignored his response, bowed her head, and prayed.

* * *

Sandy was all Brad could think about since they met yesterday. He knew a large part of that attraction was that she spoke English. But as they talked, and he learned more about her life, he was drawn to her even more.

Now here they sat, in the busiest restaurant in Queretaro, and Aunt Molly was praying – out loud. He had never prayed over food before, except at Vacation Bible School years ago.

Before Auntie Molly began, Sandy glanced at him as she lowered her head. He immediately complied with the unspoken request.

He tried to focus on what was being said, but his mind raced down every alleyway in the historic district.

When she said "Amen," Brad let out a whoosh like he'd been holding his breath. He quickly glanced around.

No one was staring at them. No one acknowledged the unusual behavior. He drew in a deep breath and chuckled ever so quietly.

He glanced at Sandy. Her eyes sparkled, her

smile contagious. *She's really special.* He wanted to pull her into his arms. *Soon. One day soon.*

* * *

Throughout the meal, the waiters hovered around the table. Sandy felt like a queen as the staff answered her every question, after Brad translated, of course.

He was becoming more of a hero each minute.

During the meal they chatted about American and Mexican foods in English. Sandy watched the faces of the wait staff that hovered about. They had no idea what the three Americans were discussing but appeared interested in every word.

Brad issued warnings about where to and where not to eat, and what *not* to try. Outdoor grills with lots of flies topped the list of places to avoid.

Everyone laughed.

Brad leaned toward Aunt Molly. "Auntie M, do you mind if I call you Auntie M?" He paused until her aunt nodded.

"And you." He pointed his fork at Sandra. "You are Sandy. Sandra is much too formal a name for an adventurous personality like you."

Auntie M clapped her left hand striking the end of the cast and her fingers. "Yes. Auntie M and Sandy. Perfect."

Sandra grinned. Joshua had insisted she be called Sandra even though she preferred the more casual version. During graduation activities, he corrected her mother for calling her Sandy. That's when she knew she could no longer see him. She got her degree and freedom the same afternoon.

She might never be called Sandra again…since

Brad preferred Sandy.

A waiter brought out a tray of desserts. Sandy wished she had saved room for at least one of the treats. The chocolate torte and the strawberry mousse tempted her taste buds. The tray of goodies could have been presented at any upscale restaurant in the States, except for that tart with miniature marshmallows covered with a light-yellow sauce on crispy tortillas.

Maybe we can come back just for those delights.

Aunt Molly insisted on paying the bill. When she handed the credit card to the waiter, Brad said something to him.

The man in the white apron smiled and hurried off.

"I told him to add fifteen percent. It's the preferred method of tipping here."

"Yes, thank you. What's next?" Auntie M leaned back and sighed. She patted her tummy. "That was so good."

"We'll go down to the Casa de la Corregidora and wander back to the car. I don't want to wear you out on your first outing." As he scooted his chair back, the legs screeched across the tiles. He didn't rise.

Auntie M's credit card was returned, and she signed the receipt. She reached to the stand holding their purses with her left hand and almost toppled out of her chair. As she tried to balance herself, she lunged forward. Reaching out with her right arm, she slammed her cast into the table leg moving the heavy table several inches.

He caught her before she hit the floor.

Sandy let out a low-pitched scream.

A swarm of waiters appeared and got her back into the chair. Tears flowed down her face and she gently rubbed the sling.

Four servers surrounded her each asking frantic questions in high-pitched Spanish.

"No, no, no. I'm all right." Auntie's words didn't match the pain on her face or the water gushing down her cheeks. She leaned back in her chair and covered her face with her good hand. "Brad, tell them to go away, they're making me nervous and creating a scene."

Sandy scampered around the table and pulled up a chair beside her aunt.

Auntie M grabbed her hand with such force, Sandy thought it might disintegrate.

Brad spoke, and the waiters vanished. All except one who conversed with Brad for several minutes. Another waiter rushed over and handed Brad a paper.

"Would you mind if we went back to the car?" Her aunt's voice was laced with tears.

"Do you want to go to the hospital?" Brad's concern accented the words.

Auntie M didn't respond.

When Sandy glanced at him, his phone was at his ear, and he was babbling Spanish at a rapid rate. "*Excelente!*" He met Sandy's glance. "He's already downtown."

Brad knelt in front of her aunt. "You and Sandy are going to the hospital. We'll check out the arm to be sure everything is okay. I'll follow as soon as I can get to the car. Wait for me in the emergency room, if you finish before I arrive."

Sandy crinkled her forehead. *What was he talking about?* "You called an ambulance?"

"No, I called Felipe, my driver. He'll be here in…there he is now. Come." He pointed to the street just outside the eating area. He helped Auntie M to her feet and wrapped his arm around her back.

Half carrying her, he moved toward the corner of the restaurant where a car was waiting with the door open. With tender gentleness, he got her inside, buckled her seatbelt, and closed the door.

Sandy hurried around to the other side, avoiding cars rumbling down the street.

Brad ran around the car as Sandy got inside and handed a credit card. "Give this to the clerk at the reception desk. I'll be there as soon as I can." He closed her door, stepped forward, and spoke to the driver who slid into the front seat.

Brad gave the man some cash. Then he stood and leaned toward the back window. "Buckle your seatbelts. And Sandy, you might want to close your eyes." He winked, patted the roof of the car, and dashed back to the sidewalk.

Sandy was flung against the back of the seat as the man took off. Had he been a driver in the Indy 500? Whatever the record was for zero to sixty on a cobblestoned street in Mexico, Sandy was sure the driver broke it.

She looked out the back window to catch a glimpse of Brad. He was gone. She felt like the bungee jumper when the rope broke.

Several times, she closed her eyes as they approached an intersection at a high speed or a cluster of cars standing still. Felipe blew his horn, and the cars parted.

Auntie M leaned into the corner of the seat and moaned. Tears continued to flow down her cheeks.

Sandy had no idea where they were going or how long it would take to get there. Where ever it was it wouldn't take long, not at this rate. She recognized several stretches of the Febrero. Heading toward home.

Auntie M's left hand fell onto the seat. Sandy grabbed it. "Oh, Heavenly Father, help us. Give the doctors wisdom for an accurate diagnosis. Help Aunt Molly's pain."

No more words came. She groaned in that special communication between Father and child that is only understood by the Superior One.

The car came to a screeching stop in front of the covered doorways of Star Medica.

"Here. We here." Felipe hopped out of the car and ran to Aunt Molly's door. He opened it slowly to prevent the woman from tumbling out.

Auntie M didn't respond.

Felipe stood and screamed in Spanish. Immediately, the double glass doors opened, and a gurney was shoved toward them.

Her unconscious aunt was lifted onto the cart and wheeled away.

Sandy opened her purse. "How much do I owe you?"

"No, no, no. El Señor Brad ya pagó." He handed her a business card and pointed to her aunt. "Go."

Sandy rushed to Aunt Molly's side. The attendants spoke in Spanish, probably asking questions.

She felt so alone. Lost in a world where she couldn't communicate.

* * *

Leaving the restaurant, Brad ran the fifteen blocks back to the parking garage. Even after all this time and the downhill jog, the higher altitude of the city caused him to gasp for breath.

His heart broke for Sandy. As she got into Felipe's car, she looked so forlorn. Yet she'd followed his directions exactly. She trusted him. That thought brought a sense of peace. He would go to her, help her resolve this issue.

He took the steps into the underground parking garage two at a time. Very dangerous since the steps were shorter than US risers, but he'd thrown caution to the wind.

A woman with two kids clinging to her skirt fought with the ticket machine. All she had to do was put her in ticket, pay the bill, and receive her exit voucher. Why was she having so much trouble?

Brad glanced around. Three oversized men crossed the roadway onto the landing where he stood. He stared back at the woman.

She looked at him. "*Lo siento.*"

The men stepped closer. Their faces hardened.

Brad groaned. If he'd been more careful he'd never be in this situation. Thankfully he already had his wallet out. He slipped his driver's license and a credit card into his palm. Maybe the thugs would grab the billfold and leave. As a general rule, thieves in this area weren't violent unless you resisted. He slipped his license and card into his pocket.

He needed to get to Sandy. She must be near panic at the hospital.

He couldn't help her if he was injured. He needed a protector himself.

"*¿Cuál es el problema?*" The younger of the three men walked up to the woman.

"*Papá*" The oldest child released his mother's skirt and grabbed the man's leg.

The two adults chatted in Spanish.

The other two men had stepped to the side waiting.

Brad drew a deep breath. Maybe he'd misunderstood the men's actions. But they hadn't left yet. They could still turn and attack. He took a more defensive posture, knowing full well he would give them his wallet rather than fight. But they didn't know that.

The woman reached up to the machine. "*Sí!*" She grabbed her voucher and hurried toward the other men. The man picked up the kid clinging to his leg and took the other by the hand.

No danger from him.

The party left the landing.

Brad inserted his ticket, coins, and got his voucher. He jogged through the dark interior to his car on the third level.

Chapter 4

Sandy stared at the medic pushing her aunt down the hospital hallway. "I'm sorry, I don't understand. English?"

He pointed to a desk. His jabbing motion told her that's where she should go.

She stepped to the counter as Aunt Molly was disappeared through swinging double doors.

"May I help you?" The young woman in the cubicle looked up and smiled. Her accent was pronounced, but her meaning clear.

"You speak English." Relief washed over Sandy easing the panic rising within her.

"Are you with the older woman they just brought in?"

"Yes, she's my aunt." Sandy opened her purse and took out the credit card Brad gave her. "I was told to give this to someone at the hospital."

The young Latina read through the two pages. "This is *perfecto*." She tapped the paper. "Bill here.

Ahora necesito información. Sorry. Information please."

Sandy gave Molly's name, address, and phone number. When the woman finished recording the information, she turned the computer screen toward Sandy.

"Please check to be sure everything is right."

Sandy could barely understand the broken English. But she knew hospital procedures. Once she'd read the information, Sandy nodded. "All's correct."

The woman turned the screen back toward her. "Your aunt is having x-rays right now. She'll be back in the exam room in a few minutes."

"May I..." Sandy said as the woman stood.

"If you follow me." She headed toward the double doors into the inner sanctum of the hospital.

They wove down several hallways and around multiple corners. Sandy was sure she'd never find her way out of this place. But the red *Salida* sign meant exit. She'd be fine. All she had to do was locate Aunt Molly.

Her guide stopped at a nurses' desk. "Right here. Aunt be here in five *minutos.*"

Sandy sat on the plastic chair listening to the stressed conversations in Spanish on the other side of the curtain. She had no idea what the speakers were saying, but she deduced it was sad news. Broken hearts sound the same in any language.

She glanced at the clock. She'd been here almost half an hour. The longest five *minutos* of her life.

Brad would be here soon. Sandy tipped her head

back against the wall. She had known the man for less than twenty-four hours, and she yearned for his presence. Not only for support with the language, but because he brought her protection. Never had she felt like this before. Not even with her father.

What was she going to do when she went back to the States? Or if she stayed here with Aunt Molly and Brad returned home?

She released a snort. She was already strongly attracted to Brad. How had that happened? She dated Joshua for three years before she realized he wasn't the right man for her. Was Brad just a rebound?

Nope, he was more. She couldn't put it in words, but he was special. *Lord, is he the man you have chosen for me?* She shivered.

Unfortunately, no powerful voice blasted from the heavens. But she sensed the answer to her question was *yes*.

The curtain ripped back and there he stood.

"Have you heard anything?" He pulled a chair beside her.

Sandy ducked her head hoping to hide her smile. *Not from God. Not yet anyway.*

"She should be back soon." Her heart skipped several beats when he covered her hand with his. She had to fight the urge to hug him.

The upset people in the adjacent cubicle left and they were the only people remaining in the unit. They sat in the small room listening to the clock ticking in the corridor.

Sandy stood and paced the five steps from her chair to the corner of the partition. She glanced back at Brad. "Something must be wrong. It's taking so long."

Brad smiled. "More than likely, they're verifying the payment arrangements. They might even send someone to the restaurant for proof."

"Seriously? Why don't they bring her back and let her wait here?" Frustration flowed freely in her veins.

"Hospitals here require payment before they do anything."

Sandy paced back to the chair. "Before?"

"At this hospital. If she had gone to a state hospital, she wouldn't have to do that, but she might still be waiting just to be seen. Don't worry. This is one of the best hospitals in all of Mexico." Brad leaned back and propped his right ankle on his left knee.

She took in his relaxed demeanor. "So, I shouldn't be worried about how long this is taking?"

"Nope. You keep forgetting life here moves at a much different pace." He leaned his head against the wall and closed his eyes. "Come. Sit. Rest."

She shook her head and sank onto the chair. How could she rest with this man that caused her blood to race through her veins sitting within inches of her. "What if she…"

"Don't even go there." He jolted into an upright position. "Everything is going to be fine." He turned to her.

Try as she might, Sandy couldn't tear her gaze from Brad. He reached around her shoulders and drew her toward him. Her heart thundered as he moved closer. She closed her eyes and awaited his lips moving onto hers. She felt his breath against her cheek.

The gurney bearing Auntie M appeared. "*Lo siento por el retraso.*" A nurse guided the gurney into the cubicle. Another nurse helped Aunt Molly onto the bed.

Sandy pulled away from Brad. "English?"

"Sí. We did x-rays. All is fine. She go home." The tall woman in a white nurses' outfit from the 1950's smiled.

Brad rattled off questions in Spanish.

The uniformed nurse fired back answers.

More questions and answers were exchanged. Sandy understood none of it.

"Okay, here's the scoop. Nothing is broken or damaged. Auntie M badly bruised her arm. The cast saved her from further injury. They're going to give her some pain pills and medications to reduce swelling. You can put an icepack on her elbow, but it may or may not help."

"What's she allowed to do?"

The nurse responded in Spanish. She rattled on and on, her arms flailing as spoke.

Sandy studied Brad's face for signs of worry.

Brad nodded. "She's to take it easy for a few days. While the arm's swollen, it will be painful. Once it settles down she'll be back to normal. They'll delay taking the cast off for another week."

"I understood *all* of that." Auntie M said from the bed.

Brad laughed. "Can't pull anything over on you, can I?"

"Ella puede ir en cualquier momento que está listo." The nurse set a paper on the bed beside Auntie M.

"*Costo*?" Her aunt stared at the nurse.

Brad offered Auntie M his hand. "It's been taken care of."

Her aunt stiffened and jerked her hand back. "You?"

"The restaurant." He offered his hand again.

"Fine." She accepted his offer of assistance. "I insist you stay for dinner. We're going to have pizza again."

"Or if you get to feeling better, we could go to Emilia." Brad's eyes sparkled as he helped her aunt from the bed and paused for her to slip into her shoes.

A nurse hurried over and helped Auntie M into a wheelchair. Brad looked over the nurse's head and gave Sandy a reassuring smile.

She thought her heart would flip over. This man was triggering responses she hadn't felt – ever. Why would a simple smile like that set her nerves sparking?

As the nurse guided her aunt from the cubby, Brad reached out and pulled Sandy to his side. His arm lingered on her shoulder. To keep from toppling, she wrapped her arm around his waist.

Auntie M twisted in the chair as they moved along. "I'm sure my pain pills are working. I've wanted to go to that restaurant for months."

"Feisty, isn't she?" Brad whispered into Sandy's hair.

Sandy nodded. She had never wanted anyone to

kiss her before, but she did now. Why would she want that? Joshua told her she was a lousy kisser. Such a comment from Brad would break her heart.

* * *

Brad was amused Sandy didn't let him finish their kiss. Not many girls today would have withdrawn with a red face when Auntie M returned to the cubby. In fact, many would have delighted in being *caught*. Another thing that intrigued him about this woman.

He kept his arm around her shoulders. When she wrapped her arm around his waist, his joy multiplied. It felt so right for them to link up like this. A simple gesture, yet one that made him feel they were a couple.

Never before had such a thought flashed through his mind. *Marry? Permanent? Exclusive?*

Yes, he wanted to marry her. Now, how could he convince her?

As they walked through the long halls of the hospital, he began to plan his strategy. He'd take Sandy and Auntie M to San Miguel next weekend, then to Guanajuato the next week. When they got to the famous red step in the alley, he'd kiss her in front of everyone and propose marriage.

It was risky going so fast, but he would be in Mexico only another couple of months. If the equipment was delivered sooner, he could be here a little as three weeks. He didn't want to return to the States without her.

He pulled her closer to him. He wanted her by his side from now on.

If all went as planned, by the end of the month

he could call his mother and tell her he had found The One for him. He would tell her Sandy was from California.

Of course, that would trigger a whole new set of reservations with his mother. Would he be happy with someone so liberal and such a free-thinker? That would be followed with her endless questions. Where would they live? Could he make enough money to afford a wife? Could she cook?

They exited the hospital.

"I'm parked over there." He pointed to the parking lot to the right.

"I'll stay with Aunt Molly." Sandy dropped her hand from his waist.

It was logical, normal for her to wait here. He didn't want to leave her even for a moment.

"I'll be right back." He dropped his hand from Sandy's shoulder and sprinted to his car.

He *had* to convince her to marry him.

On the drive to her house, Auntie M chatted away like a kindergartener home from the first day of school. Sandy had sat in the backseat. Probably the best place for her since all he wanted to do was hold her hand and steal kisses and traffic lights.

"Do you like to work jigsaw puzzles?" Auntie M interrupted his thoughts.

"Absolutely. Haven't done one in years, but if I recall correctly, I'm pretty good." He glanced at Sandy in the rearview mirror.

She was smiling.

"Sandy brought me a thousand-piece puzzle. You can help us put it together. We've got a little time before dinner."

Brad laughed. "I may be good, but I don't think I'm *that* fast."

"Oh, you silly boy. We won't finish it today. With luck, we'll get the border done. You'll have to come help us work on it this week." The older woman leaned her head back and closed her eyes.

Brad grinned as he turned onto their street. His plan would work more smoothly if Auntie M decided to be a matchmaker. Sandy didn't stand a chance of refusing him.

Once the puzzle featuring candy wrappers from the 1980s was dumped onto the kitchen table, Auntie M decided it was time to rest. She retreated to the recliner in the living room, and was soon snoring.

"I haven't worked a puzzle since the summer after I graduated." Brad found the last corner piece. He moved his hands over the piles of pieces stopping frequently to flip bits right side up and put everything into a single layer. Edge pieces went to Sandy.

She put sections together almost as fast as he could get the tiny squares to her.

"And now you can start again." Sandy reached over and put another border unit in place.

"What are your plans now?" He tapped his piece against the glass table and held his breath. Afraid of her answer.

"In July, I'll need to go home and find a job. That's when most school districts will be hiring. Until then, I'll stay and help Aunt Molly get on her feet." She didn't look up from the puzzle.

"So, where do you want to work?" He pretended

to try to fit the piece in his hand into the border.

"I'm thinking northern California. I'm certified in the state already, so that would be the easiest. I've thought of other places but getting certified say in Colorado or Tennessee is more complicated." She added to the border.

Not limited to California. Good news! He added three pieces to the border and pulled out a piece that would fit into the Snickers section.

"So, what are your plans after you finish your doctorate?"

He noticed her hand shake slightly. She was concerned about his answer too. If she wasn't, he was going to pretend she was. Oddly, it made him feel complete.

"I've already been offered jobs from two car companies who want their building projects to meet American standards. I'm not sure what I'm going to do. Those jobs would require long amounts of time out of the country. After a year here, I'm not sure I want to do that again. But on the other hand, I have become almost fluent in Spanish."

Sandy nodded.

Brad looked up at her. "Have you ever thought of working outside the country?" *Let's just get obvious as to what I'm thinking!* He wanted to smack himself.

"I'm like you. Sounds exciting, but language is a real problem." She gathered the pieces for Mild Duds.

He wanted to kiss her. As his wife, she would be open to a move internationally. Well, maybe she would. And for now, that was good enough.

"How are you kids doing with that puzzle?" Auntie M walked into the kitchen.

"Just fine. Almost have the border together. Come help us find the last few pieces." Sandy fixed her gaze on him as she talked.

He reached over and squeezed her hand.

A wide smile spread across Sandy's face and her eyes sparkled.

For the next hour the three put together sections of M&Ms, 5th Avenue, and Mallo Cup. Sandy found the letters for Planters, Mike and Ike, and Bazooka. Auntie squealed with delight each time she matched two pieces.

Brad enjoyed the time. While he started looking for pieces, he peeked up at Sandy. Only to discover she was watching him. Several times they locked gazes and smiled. Like when he was a kid sharing secrets with his brother.

Her reaction was simple and natural. A response that could last a lifetime. His joy at her glances surprised him.

"I'm getting hungry. Can we go eat now?" Auntie M scooted her chair back.

"Are you sure you're feeling up to it?" Brad studied the older woman's face. He could see she was still in pain.

Auntie M stood. "Yes, sir. I certainly am."

"Are you sure? You did have a rather nasty fall just a few hours ago." Sandy pushed some of the puzzle away from the edge of the table.

"I'm better. Not perfect, but better. And I really do want to go to."

Brad shot Sandy a questioning glance. She

nodded.

"Okay, then. Let's go." Brad stood and started for the door.

Sandy's aunt joined him, but Sandy lagged behind.

Brad loved the little things she did for her aunt. Sandy let the older woman think she ruled the roost. All along, Sandy was the one in charge. He sensed Auntie M knew exactly what was happening and didn't mind a bit.

Chapter 5

At the restaurant, they strode down the long, arched foyer into the main dining room. Plants, mostly ferns, lined the room made from deep red bricks.

Sandy smiled when Brad took Auntie M's hand and tucked it into his elbow. She obviously loved the attention.

When they sat, Brad turned to the waiter. *"Menús en inglés por favor."*

Sandy didn't know much Spanish, but she did know he asked for English menus. Why did that please her so much? It was a logical thing to do, but the way he did it showed great compassion for her shortcomings.

His treatment of her was so different from her past experiences. Joshua's request would have been because that's what *he* wanted. And others she dated were also focused on themselves and couldn't care less about others in the group.

Yep, she'd marry Brad tomorrow if he asked. She really hoped this relationship would go somewhere. If it did, it would have to be soon. Brad was scheduled to go back to the States in six to eight weeks. *That's less than two months!*

* * *

Brad was surprised Auntie M had almost as much trouble with Spanish as Sandy. However, she did live in a gated community of retired American expatriates. Her need to speak a language other than English to survive was limited.

With limited Spanish, Auntie M would never integrate into the Mexican lifestyle. But did retirees need to become semi-Mexican? Probably not. She would just be a tourist on permanent vacation.

After a bit of struggle with decisions, orders were placed. Same in every country. Women can never decide what they want to order at a restaurant. He ordered a brick-oven pepperoni pizza cooked.

"Auntie M, do you want to go to San Miguel next weekend?" He put the black cloth napkin in his lap.

She almost bounced in her chair but didn't move her arm. "That would be wonderful. The more sightseeing the better."

"Great. Here's my plan. We'll do San Miguel next week, then Guanajuato the next weekend. Those are the two big tourist towns in this area. After that there's Mexico City and the coast for beaches." *And my marriage proposal in two weeks.*

Aunt Molly put her left arm on the table and drummed her fingers. "We're taking all your free time."

"Aww. But you forget, you don't speak Spanish." He winked at Sandy. Would she think that's the only reason he wanted to be around them? Surely not, after his almost-kiss at the hospital. But women could be unpredictable. "And besides, I enjoy your company."

"Oh, good reply, my boy. Good reply." Auntie M chuckled.

A basket of bread was delivered to the table. The hard buns were similar to French baguettes in texture and taste. The rolls were his favorite, and one of the main reasons he liked this restaurant.

"So what do you think of my plan?" He looked directly at Sandy.

She nodded and opened her mouth to reply. But she didn't get a chance before Auntie M spoke up again.

"I think that's wonderful." The older woman cut a chunk of a roast potato and popped it into her mouth.

"Good. I'll call Felipe and get the trip to Guanajuato on his schedule. The town is about an hour and a half from here. But the streets in the town are unbelievably confusing. Not a place I want to drive." Brad took his last bite of brick-oven baked pizza and pushed his plate to the corner of the table. By the time he pulled his phone from his pocket, the dishes had been removed.

He chatted in Spanish on the phone as the two women finished eating.

He covered the phone with his hand and turned to Auntie M. "We have a problem. Felipe is scheduled for weekend after next and the week after that. But he is open next weekend. Do we want to schedule him?" His heart thundered. *I can't propose next week. It's too soon.*

"I'll be healed by then." Auntie M's excitement bubbled through her words. "Tell him next weekend will be fine."

Brad complied with her wishes. "Okay, all set. I'll call and get a guide. Like I said, the town is confusing."

Sandy leaned on her elbows. "Will it be a walking tour?"

"It will. Is that all right?" He couldn't get to special step without walking.

"No problem. Just curious." Sandy's cheeks reddened.

She's so cute when she's embarrassed. But why would walking cause that response? He'd have to ask her later.

Auntie M yawned. She quickly covered her mouth, unsuccessfully hiding the action.

"It's about time to get you home." He patted Auntie M's left arm and handed his credit card to the waiter.

Auntie M's smile seemed forced as she nodded. She cradled the sling as she started to get up.

* * *

Sandy stood beside her aunt. "I can't believe you came to dinner tonight. It's been a long day."

"I wouldn't have missed this for the world. But I am getting tired and need to go home."

"We're on the way." Brad joined the two women. "I'm going to get the car, so take your time. I'll meet you at the front door." He took off in a jog down the foyer.

"I hope I didn't ruin your evening." Aunt Molly squeezed Sandy's arm.

"You didn't." Sandy patted her aunt's hand.

"I can see in your eyes that you like that young man."

"I do. He speaks English." Sandy chuckled.

Auntie M swatted Sandy's arm. "I wasn't born yesterday."

Sandy swung open the restaurant door and led her aunt to Brad's car. "And he's a good guide and likes sightseeing."

As her aunt got into the car she glanced back at Sandy. "I know these things."

* * *

Brad escorted the two women into the house.

Auntie M went straight to her bedroom.

Brad lingered by the door. "Do you have a phone so I can call you rather than go through Auntie M?" He hoped he could call her throughout the day. Touch base and let her know how much he cared.

Sandy shook her head. "While in California, I had a stalker. When I came here I canceled the service. I'll get a new one when I return. Cell phone numbers are harder to discover." She averted her eyes.

A stalker! Anger surged through him. How could anyone do that to Sandy? "Are you okay? Are you safe? Do you know who is stalking you? Does he know where you are?" He threw the questions out much too fast. He pulled her into his arms. He wanted to protect her from this person.

"I'm fine. Only my parents know where I am. Everyone else was told I'm visiting Aunt Molly. Aunt's names don't include last names. And no one knows where she is." She laid her head against his chest.

"Are you planning to go back to LA?" He'd have to go with her, if that's what she wanted to do. But she'd need someone to stand up for her, to protect her back.

"No. When I came here, I sold most of my stuff, sent the rest to my mom's, and for all practical purposes, I disappeared from the face of the earth." She drew a deep breath and stepped away from him. "That's why I'll be looking for a job somewhere other than LA or even San Diego. I heard he'd taken a job there."

"And you're sure he doesn't know you're here." Brad glanced down the street expecting to see a mysterious figure lurking in the shadows.

She chuckled. "I'm sure. Don't let your imagination run away with you. Joshua wouldn't hurt me, he just wanted to own me."

Brad shook his head. "When I leave, be sure to lock the door."

She leaned against the door frame. "I will."

"I'll give your aunt a call tomorrow. Maybe we can have dinner." Could she hear the ardent hope in his voice?

She cocked her eyebrows. "I could cook dinner. Can't rival the food we had today, but I am a pretty good cook."

"I bet you are." He stepped toward her planning to run his fingers through her hair and kiss her. He halted. If he waited until Saturday, they could have their first kiss on the red step that part of the legend of Romeo and Juliet of Mexico. He believed she was enough of a romantic to like that. "I'll call tomorrow."

He turned and dashed out the door.

* * *

Sandy held onto the open door until he drove away. She thought he was going to kiss her, but he backed away. *What happened?* Obviously, he had no idea how much she wanted his kiss.

She eased the door closed and went to check on Aunt Molly.

* * *

Brad called Auntie M's number Sunday morning. No answer. *Guess lunch is out.*

After leaving a message that he'd call later in the day, he headed to the school to check the work done at his science building. He could check that off his to-do list and leave more time in the afternoon to visit Sandy.

The tiles had been put in the third-floor bathrooms Friday. He hadn't noticed if the grout had been put in.

The flooring job looked perfect. The workers had done a beautiful job with the grout, and had cleaned up behind themselves. He was building a skilled workforce.

When he turned the faucet in the sink, no water flowed out. He rushed to the first floor and turned on the water in the men's room. Only a trickle dribbled out, but there was no pressure.

Why hadn't he checked the system himself? His

foreman verified the flow rates. Another issue to cover tomorrow.

Wait! Friday, he'd washed his hands on the first floor right after the water had been turned on. He had no problem with volume or water pressure then. What had happened in the last thirty-six hours?

The above-ground tank had to be nearly empty or somewhere the pipes were blocked. Otherwise water would flow due to gravity.

He rushed to the base of the tower and checked the gauges. The arrow indicating volume of water in the tank pointed to the red danger zone. Empty? How could that be? Where were the thousands and thousands of gallons normally stored in the tank? Somewhere on campus, there had to be a massive leak.

He went to the pumphouse adjacent to the tower. Were the pumps moving the water from the well to the tank?

Using the campus code, he punched in the numbers for the lock and swung the door open. The two pumps were humming. *Good.* He walked behind the machinery and touched the cover of the nearest pump. He jerked his hand back. Hot! *How long has it been running to create that much heat?*

As he walked out of the control room, two security guards greeted him with their guns drawn and pointed at his heart.

Chapter 6

Brad threw his hands into the ai,r then froze. *"Soy Brad Andrews. Yo trabajo aquí."*

"*Es el tipo de la ciencia. Él está bien,*" one of the guards said.

Both men holstered their weapons.

Brad explained the problem as best he could. Would they understand terms like water mains and service valves?

He asked if they had seen water running in the road anywhere on campus.

The guards shook their heads. They had noticed nothing out of the ordinary, especially water flowing anywhere.

Somewhere on campus a million gallons of water was doing some serious damage. But where?

As they walked back to the security office, Brad called the chancellor.

While waiting for his boss, he'd take one of the golf carts and check the grounds outside the science building and the Administrative offices. One guard would check around the men's and women's dorms. And the other would investigate the classroom buildings. Everyone grabbed a walkie-talkie and headed out.

Surely that much water would be running out somewhere.

Brad circled the admin facility. No leaks anywhere. He started toward the science building when a glimmer on the back side of the men's dorm caught his eye. *A geyser*. That had to be the leak.

His radio squawked. *"El agua está saliendo del suelo detrás del edificio de los hombres."* The man screamed into the walkie-talkie.

Brad turned the golf cart so sharply it almost tipped over. With the pedal to floor, he raced down the hill to the edge of the campus and the men's dorm. He jumped the curb and sped across the grass to be back of the building.

The geyser sprayed three feet into the air and rippled into a pool approximately five feet across. It looked terrible, but if it was caused by a broken pipe, the problem could probably be easily fixed.

Last week, the delay would have churned his stomach. But now, it just gave him more time to get to know Sandy. Not a bad prospect. He smiled.

Problem found. Now the work begins.

After giving instructions to keep everyone away from the back of the building which wouldn't be hard since there were no construction workers on campus on Sunday afternoon, Brad ran back to the water tower and turned off the main service valve. He watched the gauge slowly rise indicating water flowed into the tank and not out.

The president pulled up just as Brad returned to the men's dorm. They went to the pool and waited for the water to flow out of the trench one of the guards made.

As the pipe was exposed Brad pointed. "There. The flange wasn't installed properly. Pressure from water filling the line caused it to blow. Not a hard problem to fix."

The campus president rubbed his hand down his face. "I thought we ran a test to be sure everything was okay before the water was turned on."

"Should have. I bet that test wasn't done." Brad knew this statement just cost someone their job.

It pained him to think of one of the supervisors losing their income. Maybe the culprit would only be demoted.

The sun dropped low in the sky casting long shadows across the road.

The president started toward the front of the building. "Since it's getting dark, we're not going to get anything done tonight. I'll call the contractors and have them meet us here at eight in the morning. Good for you?"

"Yes, sir." Brad returned the golf cart to the security office and walked up the hill to his car. His stomach growled. He hadn't eaten since breakfast.

As he left campus heading to Buffalo Wild Wings, he pulled his phone from his pocket. He needed to call Auntie M and Sandy. He phoned but no one answered.

After he left the restaurant, he called again. Still no answer. *Time to leave a message.* "Sorry I missed you. We had an emergency at the school, and I've been tied up all day. I'll try to call tomorrow."

The message left him feeling empty. He wanted to see Sandy tonight, but that wasn't a possibility. Maybe he should buy that cute little blonde a pre-paid phone.

Wow, what a day.

* * *

Sandy sat at the kitchen table working on the puzzle.

Brad had called and left a message while she and Auntie M were in church. He said he'd call later, and now it was already dark. She hoped he'd call sooner and come over for dinner. But he hadn't.

She'd met him only three days ago and had no right to expect to see him daily. Yet, it seemed she had known him forever. Maybe she should call him. She laughed aloud. She didn't have a phone and his phone number was on Auntie M's phone. Tomorrow she could drive out to the new campus and find him. That would never happen. Had she become a stalker?

When they got home from church, Aunt Molly went straight to bed. She got up about four. It had been a lonely afternoon. She was alone, didn't know how to get English stations on the TV, and didn't have a book to read. Mid-afternoon she started working on the puzzle and that helped pass the time.

All she could think about was Brad. What was he doing? Had he even thought about her and Aunt Molly? Would he ever call again?

When he left yesterday, she thought something

special had developed between them. Was she so desperate for romance, she imagined the whole thing?

She sighed and put another piece into the jigsaw puzzle.

"Sounds like you might be a bit bored." Aunt Molly stood in the archway into the living room.

"Are you feeling better?" Sandy jumped to her feet.

"Not really." She rubbed the sling. "I don't care what the doctors said, something's still wrong with my arm."

"What can we do? Do you need to go to a specialist?" She guided her aunt to the table and dropped into the seat beside her.

"I don't know. But this much pain isn't normal. Maybe I just overdid things yesterday. It hurts more today — a lot more. If it's not better in a day or so, we'll make an appointment." She leaned forward and put a piece of the puzzle into place. She had trouble turning the piece with her left hand so it would fit into the opening in the center of a Clark bar. Her injured arm remained in her lap.

The effort seemed to drain her aunt's energy.

"What would you like for dinner?" Sandy wanted to take the focus off the puzzle.

"Would you mind pizza again? I love the ones from Gregory's. Can't seem to get enough of the stuff." Aunt Molly talked as she moved pieces of puzzle around on the table but made no attempt to put any into place.

Sandy laughed. "Is that the only thing you ate before I came?"

Aunt Molly grinned. "Pretty much. That guy and his wife had a pizza shop in Chicago before they came here. And you know there's nothing better than authentic Chicago-style deep dish. Between those and the tacos from the little shop around the corner I've survived."

"Did you and your friend ever take those cooking lessons like you planned?"

"Nope. Never found a school that would teach us anything besides tacos and enchiladas. I can follow a recipe." Auntie M chuckled. "Ellen likes pizza, too. Let's invite her over."

"Sounds like a good idea." Maybe her friend would distract Auntie M from her pain. *Besides, I want to meet this woman who convinced Aunt Molly to move down here.*

They ordered the pie and waited. Ellen walked up the sidewalk just as the pizza was delivered.

Sandy had set plates, drinks and silverware on the coffee table. With the puzzle covering the kitchen table, this was the best alternative.

Auntie M didn't get out of the recliner when Ellen came into the house. "Forgive me for not getting up, but I've reinjured my arm and I moving is difficult."

"Oh, you poor dear. No wonder I haven't seen you at the clubhouse lately. And is this your niece?" The woman who could pass for fifty stared at Sandy.

Wonder what miracle cream she uses to erase her wrinkles. It wasn't normal for a woman in her late sixties not to have at least one.

"Sandy Wilcox, Ellen Madison." Auntie M's

introduction was short and sweet.

Sandy put the box of pizza on the coffee table and shook hands with the guest. "So glad to meet you."

"Your aunt is so much fun." Ellen smoothed her dark slacks. Her flowered top barely touched her waist. If she raised her arms, her tummy would show.

Auntie M snorted. "The life of the party." Her sarcasm wasn't lost on anyone.

"But honey, you've been injured. It just takes time to get back in the groove. Gregory's pizza. My favorite. Thanks for inviting me." She sat on the couch and reached for a plate.

"Before we eat, let's pray." Auntie M bowed her head and offered thanks for the food.

Sandy remained standing for the prayer. After the amen, she got a plate, nabbed the two largest pieces of pizza, and handed it to her aunt.

Ellen had reached for one of the pieces, but Sandy was quicker. For some reason, the act of giving her aunt the largest pieces gave her great pleasure. If Brad was here, he would have offered Auntie M the entire pizza. And she would have taken the two smallest pieces.

If Brad was here... Why hadn't he called? Had he had enough of these two Americans? Did he get his language fix and didn't need her anymore?

"How did you reinjure your arm?" Ellen bit the tip of her slice.

"I bumped it against a table leg while touring the historic district."

"Then you had that long drive home. That must

have been awful." Their guest picked a slice of pepperoni off the pizza and plopped it in her mouth.

"We stopped by the hospital on the way. I only bruised it." Auntie M tried to make light of the pain.

"It's a shame Roger Oxley isn't here. He could make it right in a jiffy." Ellen poured a can of Coca Light over the ice in a glass.

"What's he up to now?" Aunt Molly put her empty plate on the end table and leaned back in the recliner.

"He got a big promotion. He's head of orthodontics at Southwestern Medical School in Texas."

Sandy cocked her head. "How could an orthodontist help Aunt Molly?"

Ellen shot her a glance that would have melted a candle. "He's an excellent surgeon. He's been known to do miracles."

Aunt Molly straightened and grinned at Sandy. "She means orthopedics."

Ellen turned toward Auntie M. "Sorry. I'm always getting those two mixed up."

Not if you needed one to work on you. One glance from her aunt, and Sandy stopped the smile creeping across her face.

Conversation turned to college classmates. Almost every sentence began with *Whatever happened to…* or *Who was it that…*

Sandy dropped out of the conversation fast, yet she watched her aunt closely. Auntie M was enjoying the reminiscing. Only the occasional motion of slipping her hand under the sling and holding her arm at a different angle indicated the pain was still there.

Sandy busied herself by clearing away the pizza box and plates, making coffee, and offering the remaining chocolate chip cookies to the two women.

Brad had enjoyed the cookies just two days ago. Or was it yesterday? It's a wonder any were left. Just thinking of him being in their house warmed her heart.

Tomorrow she'd bake again. Maybe sugar cookies.

For the second time tonight, she thought she heard Auntie M's phone ringing. A faint sound off in the distance. She knew it was because of her desire to talk to Brad that she was imaging the jingle. Aunt Molly's phone was always in a pocket inside her sling.

Ellen had finally had enough reminiscing, food, and coffee. "This has been such fun. We need to do it again sometime, soon. I forget how much fun you are." She stood and went to Aunt Molly, gave her a hug, and headed for the door.

"Did you drive?" Sandy asked before they reached the entrance. She didn't see a car at the curb.

"Heavens no, child. I only live two houses down the street." She waved at Auntie M and dashed out.

When Sandy returned to the living room, she looked at her aunt. "Two doors down, and this is the first time she's been here, or even called, since I arrived. What kind of friend is that?"

"I don't think our friendship has grown since college. But occasionally it's fun to visit past times."

"True." Sandy thought of her friends from UCLA. When they saw her again after several years, their first question would be *What happened to Joshua?*

"But, take my word for it, it's not a good idea to move down the street from a friend expecting the relationship to pick up where it left off." Regret dulled her words.

"Who's this Roger?" Sandy sat in the spot on the couch still warm from Ellen.

"He's a really nice guy. I introduced him to my roommate Wilma. They fell in love. Roger and Willy. She died a couple of years ago from cancer." Her aunt scooted to the edge of the recliner.

That's two strikes on getting her focused on something positive.

Auntie M leaned forward and eased out of the chair. "Might not be a bad idea to give him a call. I'll see what I can do tomorrow. Right now, I'm going to bed." She reached the staircase and turned. "You did a great job of hosting tonight. Thank you."

"You're more than welcome." *But don't invite that woman back for a while. She's a hard pill to swallow.*

Before heading to her bedroom, Sandy tidied the downstairs.

"Sandy! Sandy, come here," Aunt Molly screamed from upstairs.

Sandy ran up the steps two at a time. When she reached the second floor, she struggled to catch her breath.

Auntie M was standing in her doorway.

"Are you okay?" Sandy gasped.

"He called twice. I left my phone upstairs, and he called twice." She waved her phone in the air like that would change reality.

"Brad?"

"Yes. I'll call him back."

"Why don't you wait until tomorrow? It's getting a little late tonight."

Or give me your phone and I'll call him.

"Wonder what time he goes to work?" Auntie M retreated into her bedroom…with her phone.

Chapter 7

By Tuesday morning, Sandy's emotions were flying high. Brad had come over for dinner last night. They had worked on the puzzle getting it about half finished.

Auntie M hadn't participated on the jigsaw project. She went to her room right after supper.

Sandy and Brad had joked, laughed, and flirted. Several times, Brad held her hand and gazed into her eyes. Then he would kiss her fingertips, grin, and release her hand by flaring his fingers like a rocket explosion at a fireworks show. Did he have any idea the pyrotechnics he set off within her? His tease sent electricity shooting to every inch of her skin. She'd never had a reaction like this before and had no idea how to control it.

She had purposely put him in situations where he could kiss her. But he hadn't.

This morning as she was praying for him, she realized how foolish she'd been. Because she wanted Brad to kiss her, she'd lowered her standards. Her behavior wasn't appropriate for a child of God. She could do better.

She smelled bacon. Quickly she got dressed and headed downstairs to join Auntie M.

"Good morning, Sunshine." Aunt Molly's greeting made Sandy smile.

"You sound happy today. Is your pain better?"

"Not at all. But I'm going to do something about it." She lifted the bacon from the pan and put it on the paper towels to drain. Then she cracked two eggs into the grease.

"And what's that?" Sandy put silverware and drinks on the coffee table. They had to finish that puzzle soon if they ever wanted to eat in the kitchen again.

"Today, I'm going to have some more x-rays done. Then I'm going to send them to Roger Oxley in Dallas. I'm also having an MRI to send to him. He'll tell me what to do to get rid of the pain." She flipped the eggs and turned the burner off.

"When did you decide all this?"

"Last night while you were getting ready for Brad. I called Roger yesterday morning. I guess I should say Doctor Oxley. And he called me back after his office hours. He was so cute. He asked if I was the Molly Davenport who had introduced him to Wilma Martin. Was I that crazy girl who decorated the lead car for the homecoming parade with crepe paper only to discover she'd decorated the university president's car instead." Aunt Molly laughed as she put the eggs on the plates Sandy had set on the counter. "The pres. never found out who did it."

"Anyway, Roger said he'd review my x-rays and the MRI and let me know what he thinks. I'm going down today to get more pictures. Then I'll FedEx them to him. I should have answers next week." She stepped back and let Sandy take the plates to the table.

Aunt Molly stood in front of the stove, spatula in hand, gazing off into space. "If anything can be done, Roger can do it. At least, I'll know." She lowered the tool, put it on the counter, and joined Sandy at the table. "At least, I'll know."

"Auntie M, that's great. So where are you going to have these procedures done?" Sandy dreaded driving on the highway. After returning from the grocery store, she'd done all the driving. The farthest she'd ventured out was the four miles to the mall. That was enough.

"Down at Star Medica, where I had the last pictures done. I've already made an appointment and called Felipe. He'll be here at nine."

"Can I go with you?" Sandy was afraid to ask. Her aunt's independence was showing, and she thought Auntie M might say *no*.

"Of course. Isn't that why you're here? To help me out. You'll need to grab your English Paper Piecing, so you'll have something to do. This may take a while."

"No problem. Everything's in my tote. I can be ready in two minutes."

They ate quietly. Sandy noticed Auntie M gazing off into space again. Something was bothering her. But her aunt didn't talk.

As they were putting the dishes into the dishwasher, Sandy stopped. "Okay, what's got you fretting?"

"Nothing." Aunt Molly's response was too quick.

"Wrong answer. What's really bothering you?" Sandy led her aunt to the kitchen table and the puzzle.

"Well…" The older woman moved some pieces around on the table. "I'm thinking if anything can be done, I'll go back to the States for treatment."

"Makes sense. And…" Sandy knew there was more.

Auntie M looked up at her. "If I go back for treatment, I'm going to move back."

"Wow, that's a major decision. Are you sure?" Sandy watched her aunt closely.

The older woman folded her arms across her lap and sighed. "My expectations of life in Mexico have fallen flat. I thought Ellen and I would become close again, but the opposite has happened. There's nothing here I can't do on vacation. I can always return for short visits. Without friends or family, there's no need to stay."

Sandy sat for a few minutes, pushing puzzle pieces around on the table and shooting arrow prayers toward heaven. "If that's the case, shouldn't you move back to the States anyway?"

Auntie M lifted her head and smiled. "I was planning to return as soon as my lease was up in November, but I see no need to wait any longer."

Sandy looked up in surprise. "So…what are you thinking?"

"What do you think about the first of May. That's five weeks. We should be able to get everything done by then." Auntie M smiled broadly.

She's already planned this out.

Even in her excitement, Aunt Molly didn't move her arm. "We can do some sightseeing, get stuff packed, and decide where to go."

"You don't even know where you want to go? The United States is a pretty big place. I'd think you'd want to go back to the Sedona area." Sandy's stomach churned with the thought of leaving in five weeks.

It shouldn't shock her. She was planning to stay just a couple more months anyway. But somehow the thought of setting a moving date for Aunt Molly upset her.

"I'll talk to my friend, Amy, in Arizona. She can get me a storage unit to send my belongings to. But, Sandy...there were reasons I was so willing to leave." Her aunt looked the out the back window toward the pots of yellow flowers on the patio.

Sandy felt her face redden. *Of course, there was. You're a maverick, but not foolish.* "Well, I think we should start planning."

Aunt Molly patted Sandy's arm. "Thank you for understanding."

During wait times at the hospital the two discussed their plans. Auntie M had a long list of places she wanted to visit before leaving Mexico. As she babbled on about different sites, Sandy knew they would never go to most of them. Auntie M's pain level was too high to do much traveling. *Let the woman dream.*

What was Sandy going to do about Brad? He would be going back to the States about the same time. The chill of emptiness swept over her. She'd had such hopes for a future with him, but time was against them.

Trust in God. Enjoy the time she had remaining and don't cry about what might have been. If God wanted her to have a long-term relationship, He'd work it out.

"Auntie M, let's not say anything to Brad until we've made definite plans."

Her aunt studied her much too long. "No problem."

* * *

All Brad's phone calls were finally paying off. Yesterday, a shipment of dry erase boards arrived. His first delivery of equipment was coming this afternoon. His boss had told him once the first box came, others would follow quickly.

Timing was unbelievable. He'd spent all day yesterday overseeing the repairs to the water system. Now, that problem was resolved. Tests showed the separated flange had been the only problem. Soon the landscape would have grass back in place and no one would be the wiser that they'd lost more than a million gallons of water.

Except the treasurer when he paid the bill.

For three weeks, he'd been hoping for everything to show up on his doorstep. Now that it was coming, and Sandy was in his life, he didn't want things to happen so fast. Everything was either feast or famine. All the time in the world to fall in love, but no one to invest in, or no time at all and

Sandy.

If all his orders arrived in the next two weeks, he'd have very little time away from campus. He was going to have to control this flood of projects.

He had already installed the security system for the third floor where most of the equipment would be installed or stored. With permission from the president, he could have all the deliveries moved there and set the alarms at night. The security guards would need to be made aware the system was activated. That would give him some control of the chaos that was coming.

This Saturday he was taking the girls to Guanajuato. Next Saturday he might have to work. He needed to get the countertops, sinks, and Bunsen Burners installed, and the high-grade microscopes secured.

He'd not only have to insure the equipment was installed, he'd have to teach the workers how to do it properly. The enormity of the project came into focus.

This week all deliveries could go to the third floor. Then...then he'd be busy.

If he explained the situation to Sandy, would she understand? She would, he knew. But they had so little time to grow their relationship. As soon as this equipment and supplies were in place, he'd be heading back to Arkansas.

Don't count your chickens before they hatch. It may take months to get everything delivered.

At four, he finished his check list for the day. The morning had been spent teaching his workers how to install the newly arrived dry erase boards.

The afternoon he had supervised their work. And now all the classrooms were equipped. He was feeling good about the day's work.

He sent his crew to the Liberal Arts building to help install dry erase boards there.

He was meeting the girls for dinner then going to some meeting with them. He thought Sandy said church, but it wasn't Sunday. He'd agreed only because it meant he could spend more time with her.

He was concerned about Auntie M's pain levels which were off the charts. She tried to disguise her discomfort, but he could see it. And if he was right, it was getting worse. Surely the doctors could do something.

He needed to get on the road if he was going to make dinner on time. He set the alarms and locked the door.

A large van with three red stars on the side pulled in front of the building. The driver hopped out and rushed toward him. "Are you Brad Andrews?"

Brad nodded. The man about his age spoke in English. Who was he?

He turned and waved to his passenger who got out and started toward the back of the truck. "I'm Mike Johnson. We've got some stuff for you." He started toward his partner.

"Stuff?" Brad was still in shock at the man's perfect American English.

"Do you have a delivery entrance?"

"Follow the road to the back of the building. I'll go through and unlock the doors." He still didn't know who these men were. Hopefully they weren't muggers.

Brad got the front door unlocked before the driver started his engine. He relocked the door so he wouldn't have to come back through the building later. He dashed along the corridors to the receiving room and raised the doors.

The truck was parked against the ramp. Several boxes were already on the dock.

Brad glanced into the truck. It was fully packed. "Is all that coming here?"

"Yes sir. It arrived about noon. If it hadn't taken so long to get through customs, we'd have been here hours ago. The guys at the airport were bored and had to check out several of the boxes. Just to be sure they contained what the invoice said."

Brad stared at the shipment. It would take more than an hour to empty that truck and move everything to the third floor.

"I thought they might be looking for drugs. Funny, smuggling drugs *into* Mexico. Seemed a little backward." He shrugged. "Maybe they were looking for guns. Anyway, you're well inspected." He moved another box to the platform. "Is there anyone who can help us? We *can* unload all this ourselves, but it'll take a while."

"Yeah, sure." Brad pulled out his phone and called his crew manager. He turned back to the truck driver. "They'll be here soon."

"Where do you want this?" The helper had a dolly loaded with three boxes.

Brad needed them on the third floor, but deliveries were made to the receiving room. These men had no clearance for the third floor. He'd have to move them up himself. "In this area." He waved his hand to the section near the elevator.

His crew arrived and helped empty the truck.

Brad turned to the manager. "All these boxes need to go to the third floor. I'll go turn the alarms off."

As he walked down the hall, he pulled out his phone and called Auntie M.

"Brad, how good to hear from you." Her cheerful greeting was laced with pain.

"Maybe not. I just got a major delivery at the campus and I won't be able to make dinner." He hated to say this. Auntie M liked to go out to eat and he liked visiting Sandy. Now neither would happen.

"Oh, I'm sorry." Her voice was strained.

"Me too." He entered the office and turned off the security system. "I've got at least another two hours of work here. I'll see you tomorrow night?"

"Yes. We'll be here." Auntie M disconnected.

He returned to the receiving deck to check in the boxes. It would be a long night.

* * *

Sandy jumped to her feet as Auntie M came down the steps. Her aunt was weaker by the hour and becoming unsteady. She hadn't used her right arm since they left the hospital. The only handrail was on the right which meant she had to reach across her body with her left hand to hold on. Thankfully she knew she needed to grasp the rail rather than Sandy having to tell her to.

Once Aunt Molly sent the x-rays and MRI off to

her doctor in Dallas, she'd given in to her pain. Without a fight, the pain took over.

With a grimace, as Auntie M stepped into the living room. "Brad can't come tonight. He got a shipment that has to be taken care of. He said it would be a while, and he'd see us tomorrow."

Sandy tried not to let her disappointment show. Auntie M didn't need that reaction. "I can make sandwiches or a salad. No wait. We don't have lettuce. Okay, I can make sandwiches. Or I can run and pick up fast food."

Aunt Molly nodded. "If you don't mind, can we pass on the service tonight? I'm just not feeling well."

"Do I need to take you to the hospital?" She moved closer to her aunt.

"No, I finally broke down and took one of those pain pills the doctor gave me last weekend. It's making me a bit woozy. I'll be fine. Would you mind running over to the taco shop and getting us dinner?"

"I can. We've been there enough, they can deal with my Spanish." Sandy laughed.

Auntie M smiled. A quick ha-ha-that's-cute-but-I-hurt smile.

"Anything else you need while I'm out?"

Her aunt shook her head slightly. She pushed the button to release the leg support and closed her eyes.

Aunt Molly needed food in her stomach since she was taking meds. Sandy grabbed her purse and hurried out the door.

Chapter 8

When she woke up Wednesday morning, Sandy looked around. *Where am I?*

Aunt Molly's snoring snapped her to attention.

Last night her aunt fell asleep in the recliner almost immediately after eating two tacos. So Sandy had slept on the couch just in case she needed help.

All was well, except for the kinks and cramps from sleeping like a wadded-up blanket.

Yesterday while Auntie M was upstairs asleep, Sandy had worked on the puzzle and thought about Brad all day. Her emotions couldn't handle a repeat. She'd work on her English Paper Piecing.

She grabbed an apple from the kitchen for breakfast and went upstairs to get her tote. Before returning downstairs, she took a quick shower and changed her clothes. She felt better.

When she got downstairs, Auntie M's chair was empty. Sandy panicked until she heard the toilet flush. She put her bag of supplies on the coffee table and sat on the couch.

Auntie M maneuvered back to her chair and sank into it.

"What would you like for breakfast?" Sandy stood and headed toward the kitchen.

"Any of those tacos left?"

The response surprised Sandy. The bacon and eggs woman changed her order. "Yes, two. Want me to heat them up?"

"Please. I had a stomach ache last night after taking those pills. But once I ate tacos, it went away. I'm going to take some more..." She stopped like she'd run out of energy in the middle of her thought.

Sandy reached the kitchen archway and turned to face her aunt. "Microwave or oven?"

"Microwave, seventy seconds." The directions were issued with authority.

Sandy laughed. "Sounds like you're skilled in reheating tacos."

"I'm good at pizza too. A well-honed skill. As you can see, I survived quite well." Auntie M wiggled in the chair.

After her aunt finished eating, she coughed several times.

"Do you need your pills? Can I do something for you?" Sandy knew the sound from her aunt was attention-getting and not illness.

"I've been thinking. I can move anywhere, and you can get a job teaching anywhere. I've got money and no kids, so..." She pulled herself to a sitting position. "I've enjoyed having you in the house. When I go back to the States, I can get a house and you can live with me. For a while anyway. Until you get on your feet from your new job."

"I thought you weren't going back until November."

"I can go back any time I want. First thing would be to decide where you want to work. Then we can make plans."

That would be a great idea except Sandy hoped something developed with Brad. *Don't dash her dreams.* "I'd never thought about living anywhere outside California."

"You can teach anywhere. Might take a bit to transfer your certification, but it can be done. Think about it."

"I will." It saddened her to think of life without Brad. Maybe that was a reality she should consider. Not today.

* * *

Brad stayed at the school until almost ten last night. He'd finally gotten all the boxes inventoried and assigned to rooms. Today, he'd teach his crew how to install the cabinets, countertops and sinks for the labs. There were four classrooms with five rows of counters each. That should take some time.

Hopefully the chemical cabinets would arrive next. Once those were in place, the specialty equipment on the third floor could be connected. Then it was just a matter of moving the supplies to the right rooms.

He could see the end of the tunnel. But when he looked through that tiny hole so far away, he didn't see Sandy. With shipments arriving, his free time would be more limited. He groaned. He couldn't wait until the project was finished to date her, because then he'd be heading back to Arkansas to defend his dissertation.

Thinking of life without Sandy made his heart ache.

Deliveries wouldn't be made Saturday, so nothing would interrupt his plans for the Juliet step. He had to make the most of their time together.

Tonight, he was going to take the girls to dinner. He looked forward to seeing them again. Had he missed being with them…was it only one day?

He was concerned that Auntie M's pain wasn't easing. Maybe he could talk to Sandy about options if Auntie M gave them a chance to converse privately. He wasn't sure he had any alternatives, but he wanted to broach the subject. So many things to consider.

All day he'd been working with his crew. Two lab cabinets were installed. Gas and water hadn't been connected but the woodwork, countertops, sinks, and Bunsen burners were in place. At this rate it would take two weeks to install the cabinets.

At four o'clock, the big van with three red stars and driven by Mike Johnson, cruised past the front door. He waved to Brad as he headed to the loading dock.

Brad stared at the truck in unbelief. He was going to be late to dinner. But at least the girls didn't have a meeting to get to. After he opened the door for the delivery, he headed to the second floor to alert the crew.

If they got the boxes upstairs, he could label them with room assignments tomorrow. And still get across town to Sandy and Auntie M in time for dinner.

* * *

All day the idea of her moving niggled in the corner of Sandy's mind. When Aunt Molly said she was thinking of moving in five weeks, Sandy's stomach churned.

Now, Aunt Molly had opened the entire country as a place to settle. If Sandy could live anywhere where would that be? *Near Brad.* But where would he be in another year? His doctorate program was almost completed, Then, he'd get a job—somewhere. He'd already said he might take an international assignment.

How in the world could she discuss this with Brad? He'd think she was being pushy. Asking him to make a commitment he wasn't ready to make. Even worst, he might tell her that the decision was hers and had nothing to do with him.

She wasn't ready to fight that battle.

* * *

After what seemed forever, the shipments were secure on the third floor. Brad glanced at his watch. Six o'clock! He should be at Sandy's house by now, and with traffic he was more than an hour away.

He set the alarm, headed to his car, and jerked his phone from his pocket. He pushed Auntie M's icon. The phone rang but went straight to voice mail.

"Sandy, Auntie M, I got tied up at work. Another late delivery that had to be secured. I'm on my way and should be there within an hour. Give me a call."

A knot grew in his stomach. He should be there with them. What had happened? Why hadn't she answered? Had Auntie M hurt herself again? Were they at the hospital?

As he sped away from campus, he tried to call again. They still didn't answer.

He drove like a teenager on the road for the first time. Dashing in and out of traffic and going much too fast. He had to concentrate on the cars around him but his concern for the girls dominated his thoughts.

He had known these two women for almost a week…not even a week! They had come to mean more to him than anything in the world. He was in love with both of them. They had become family.

Something was wrong at their house. Hopefully it was as simple as a dead phone battery, but it could be as serious as another accident. Not knowing was maddening. He had to get to them.

Unbelievably, traffic thinned, and he sped down the Febraro at breakneck speeds. He glanced at the speedometer. Ninety! No, no. That was dangerous. He took his foot off the gas pedal. Elephants stampeded in his stomach. His nerves tingled. He needed to hurry.

Why wasn't Auntie M answering her phone? His speed crept up again, and he had to deliberately lift his foot. What if she'd fallen? What if she'd fallen after he should have been there? It would all be his fault.

His thoughts swirled down the what-if drain into

a cesspool of terror. His hands shook.

He swerved in and out of lanes, cutting off cars, and blasting his horn at cars going too slow. He was being a jerk. Nobody in Mexico blows their horn. They simply take control of the road.

He was completely out of control. He knew it, but Auntie M and Sandy needed him. He had to get to them. He had to hurry.

At last the gate to their *privada* came into view. The guard waved him through. Was that even safe? He'd been here almost daily, but shouldn't they check his I.D. anyway? Had someone broken into Auntie M's house and hurt the girls?

Thankfully he couldn't speed on the cobblestoned roadway. He'd never seen a kid playing in the street, but if one was to do that, tonight would be the time. He turned the corner and there was the house with her car in the carport.

They were home. He gulped air and tried to calm his nerves. Why hadn't they answered the phone?

He pulled to the curb, jumped out of the car, and ran to the house. Maybe everything was okay.

Through the glass door he watched Sandy walk across the room. She was calm, unhurried.

She opened the door. "Perfect timing."

Her smile was the most beautiful thing he'd ever seen. He wanted to pull her into his arms and hold her. But it was too soon. He'd only known her for a week. If he expressed his feelings, it might scare her. Especially since she'd had a stalker. He took her hand.

Her eyes glittered.

"I called, and you didn't answer." He wanted to yell and ask why she didn't call back.

"Auntie M left the phone upstairs. By the time I got to it, you'd left a message. And when I called back you didn't answer. I thought you might be on the road, so I left a message."

"You called?" How could that be?

"You asked me too. Wasn't that okay?" She stood beside the door her hand in his.

"You left a message?" Relief washed over him. Everything was okay.

Sandy looked completely confused. "Yes. I said Aunt Molly didn't feel well, and we would order pizza. It just arrived. I hope that's okay."

"Yes, yes. That's fine." He slipped his arm around her shoulders to pull her to him.

"Brad. Is everything alright? You look rather tense." Auntie M stood beside her recliner.

He dropped his arm, released Sandy's hand, and stepped into the living room. "Yes, ma'am. I just spent an hour in traffic, and you know how that can be."

As he walked across the room to give the older woman a hug, he pulled his phone from his pocket. There it was. New voice mail message. Why hadn't he heard her call?

He turned to Sandy. "I put my phone on silent this morning when I went to a meeting. I guess I never turned it back up. I had it in my pocket and evidently didn't notice it vibrate as I was driving."

He'd driven like a maniac. Fast and dangerous on a Mexican road. And all for nothing. He'd done some dumb things in his life and this ranked right up there with the dumbest. And he'd gotten here…he glanced at his watch…five minutes faster than normal.

That's what Sandy did to him – sent him out of control.

* * *

After dinner, Sandy cleared the coffee table.

Brad had been a nervous wreck when he arrived. Something had his nerves on edge. He said it was traffic, but she knew it was more than missing a phone call. What had he said in his message. Late shipment at work.

"How are things going on the job?" Maybe some innocent probing would produce an answer.

"It's frustrating. My equipment is finally coming in. But shipments arrive a little after four, and my crew leaves at five. We unpack the truck and haul everything up to the third floor. Then I have to inventory all those boxes."

"How many boxes?" Auntie M wiped marinara sauce off her cheek and tossed the napkin into the trash can beside her.

"The order yesterday was over a hundred boxes. The driver arrived tonight after four. They unloaded another sixty boxes. I haven't inventoried them yet."

He flinched.

Is he feeling guilty about being here?

"They've been secured, and I'll get to them first thing in the morning."

Auntie M sat up in her chair. "Why are these orders arriving so late. Why don't they bring them in the morning or early afternoon?"

"The shipment's coming in from the States. Everything is loaded in the morning, flown down. The biggest problem is getting through customs. Then it's put on a truck and shazam." His fingers flew out like a firecracker explosion. "It's delivered about four."

Sandy noted his movements as he talked to Aunt Molly. He used his hands a lot, and the muscles in his arms and chest rippled as the talked. She wanted to touch him. See if he was as taut as she imagined.

The feelings she had when she first saw him returned with a fury. Her swoon was back. Wouldn't that create a scene? She ducked her head to hide her grin. Auntie M noticed, but Brad's didn't. His back was to her. At least, she wouldn't have to explain such an odd reaction.

Brad turned to her. "Everything's all set for the trip to Guanajuato. Felipe will be here at eight. I'll drive over and leave my car here."

Sandy stared at her shoes.

"What's wrong?" Brad looked at her and jerked his head to Auntie M. "What's wrong?"

Auntie M's voice cracked. "I'm not going."

Brad spun his head around and looked at Sandy. His eyes glowed with compassion. Then he turned back to her aunt. "You're not up to the trip?"

Auntie M slowly shook her head. "I can't make it. I can hardly make it to the kitchen, and the drive would literally kill me."

Brad turned back to Sandy. "And you. Can you go?"

"Yes, she can." Auntie M blasted the words.

Brad smiled and turned back to Auntie M.

Her aunt lifted her head and tipped her chin. "Yes, she will."

No arguing. Sometimes Aunt Molly could be very bossy. Especially since Sandy had no desire to cancel!

"There's more shipments coming. So, if you girls don't mind, I'll stay and get everything done tomorrow evening, so I can relax on Saturday."

Sandy's heart sank. Yes, he should stay and get the job done, but she wanted to see him. To be close to him. *How selfish of me.*

Brad watched her.

He knew what she was thinking. She was sure of it. He knew of her ruse on the highway, and he knew her thoughts now.

"If no shipment comes tomorrow, or if I can get things done before eight, I'll call and stop over. Okay?" He focused on her.

Sandy nodded, and he smiled.

He glanced at his watch. "I should be going. Tomorrow will be busy."

"We're glad you stopped by tonight." Auntie M lowered the leg support and scooted forward.

Brad's hand flew up into a stop sign. "Don't get up. Rest."

"I'll be feeling better next week. My x-rays are in the hands of a specialist. He's going to help me." Auntie M sank back in the chair. "Maybe I can go sightseeing after that."

Brad's lips curled upward, his eyes sparkled, and his eyebrows rose slightly. "I'll look forward to it."

Sandy escorted him to the door.

"I'll see you Saturday morning at eight." He leaned forward as if he would kiss her. But he stopped.

And so did Sandy's heart. *Wonder what he'd do if I kissed him.*

Chapter 9

Saturday's weather was perfect for sightseeing and picture taking. High in the mid-seventies, slight breeze, and blue skies.

Sandy was so excited she woke up at five and was ready to go by six. She walked down the steps in the dark without turning on a light and possibly awaking Auntie M.

When Brad hadn't called last night, she prepared everything, and was ready. Her phone charged, and her drawstring bag loaded with money, credit card, and passport. Now, she waited.

She flipped on a light as she walked past the bookshelf filled with only part of Aunt Molly's collection. Her gaze settled on a guidebook on Mexico. She read the sections on Queretaro before they toured the historic section last week but had been so concerned about Aunt Molly's pain she forgot about the resource. She pulled the book out and sank on the couch to study the town she would soon tour.

The town of Guanajuato developed around silver mines in the 1550s and was built in a narrow valley between four mountain peaks. That was before the Pilgrims landed at Plymouth Rock. She couldn't find a flat section anywhere on the map. Their walking tour would be up and down hills on cobblestoned sidewalks.

Auntie M slowly descended the steps.

Sandy started to rush to her side, but Aunt Molly wore the same independent expression as on the day she went for x-rays. "You're up early."

Her aunt smiled. "I was hoping things would be better and I could tag along with you guys today."

"Good. It's going to be fun." Concern gripped Sandy's heart. Auntie M could barely walk to the car without pain overtaking her. Could she handle a day of walking?

"Can't do it. Hoping didn't make it happen." She shrugged and sat in the recliner.

Sandy was relieved.

"Once I get something done about this arm, we can go together." She plopped a pillow into her lap and rested her sling on it.

Sandy closed the book and put it on the coffee table. "That'll be great." If Auntie M stuck with the May first moving date, that would never happen. *Let her dream.*

She glanced at her aunt. Without a doubt, the older woman realized her limitations. Another disappointment for her stay in Mexico.

Sandy fixed breakfast, cleaned the kitchen, and

chatted with Auntie M until Brad finally arrived an hour and a half later. They talked about everything except Mexico and the upcoming move.

When he walked into the house, Auntie M lit up like a sparkler on the fourth of July. She rattled on in shallow conversation while Sandy gathered her fanny pack.

Brad focused on her aunt.

When Sandy moved toward the door, Brad shifted his attention to her. Her heart beat rapidly and he touched her back to guide her to the car.

"I invited Felipe's wife to join us. I hope you don't mind."

He'll be in the back seat with me! She shook her head.

"She's learning English. They're going to take the tour with us."

"That'll be fun."

"I don't want you to get bored with me." He opened the door then stepped away to speak to Felipe.

That's one thing you don't have to worry about.

She shook the hand of Maria, Felipe's wife, when introduced. The woman seemed surprised at Sandy's reaction. Hope she didn't break any protocol rules.

On the drive across the high desert Sandy was fascinated with the unusual landscape. It was relatively flat with green hills popping up occasionally. Huge cacti shrubs and dried grasses frequently covered the tan and gray dirt.

As they neared the city, everything changed. The uniformity of the plain was replaced with sharp hills and stone outcroppings. As they drew closer, multi-colored houses in the oranges, red and blues that identified Mexico were stacked on top of one another against the mountain like children's building blocks.

Sandy became a sponge, soaking in all the cultural feast before her. *And they haven't even started the tour. Auntie M would love this. If her arm gets better, they could come over and spend the night.* Sandy snapped pictures on her phone camera in rapid succession.

She was in an alternative universe. This town looked much like it did in the sixteenth century when the silver mines were in full production.

The cathedrals and churches with their baroque facades took her breath away. While touring the Templo de Valenciana, Brad closed her mouth by tipping her chin with his finger.

"I told you this would blow your socks off." He grinned.

She moved from one floor to ceiling altar to the next mesmerized with the artistic details.

They lingered over the oversized oil paintings that lined the side walls.

As they walked out of the church, their tour guide pointed to a statue at the top of a precipice. "That's our next stop."

Sandy imagined walking up the hillside. *That's at least a thousand steps.*

"And that's how we'll get there." She pointed to an incline railway.

Brad chuckled when Sandy release a whoosh.

The escort started toward the terminal. "Then

we'll walk down the hill to the Callejon de Beso and on to the Mercado Hidalgo for lunch."

* * *

Brad's heart quickened. He was hoping the guide wouldn't go into too much detail about the red Juliet's step in the alley. He'd like to tell Sandy that story after...he kissed her. He barely heard the spiel the guide gave about the statue and the view.

Finally, they started down the narrow, twisting sidewalk toward the bottom of the hill.

Sandy oohed with the closeness of the houses that seemed to be stacked on top of one another. Their descent was slow because of the cobblestones and steps. In some places, the walkway was only three feet wide. At those points, he scooted in close to this girl he'd fallen in love with. In some ways, he was disappointed that he hadn't had the time to strengthen his relationship. He wanted to profess his love on that magical step, but it was too soon.

When the guide started the story of the balconies, Brad interrupted her in Spanish. Hopefully, Sandy didn't understand. The guide smiled. "I'll continue this story later."

When the red step came into sight, Brad had trouble keeping his emotional balance. "When you get to that red step, stop. It's part of Mexican tradition."

"Okay." She was so trusting.

She stepped onto the magical step and turned to him. Anticipation made her eyes twinkle.

Brad lost control. He pulled her into his arms and kissed her. No build-up, no teasing.

Felipe clapped.

The guide stood in front of them and announced to those gathered on the small plaza. "When you kiss and declare your love on this step, you love will last forever."

Sandy looked at him with such compassion. "Forever?" Her word was barely above a whisper.

"I've fallen in love with you." He hadn't released her. He kissed her again, taking a little more time as he stroked her hair and looked deep into her eyes.

Her eagerness surprised him. Her approval removed all filters. He had to tell her. Tell her now.

"I love you." He dropped to a knee and took her hand. "Sandy Wilcox, will you marry me."

She didn't move.

His heart raced. Had he made the biggest mistake of his life? *Dummy, you should have given her time.*

Tears trickled down her cheeks. "Yes."

Brad popped to his feet and pulled her to him. His head swam, and passion burned within him. He didn't want to ever let her go.

When the crowd in the plaza began clapping and cheering, he stepped back.

The guide explained in Spanish his proposal. Felipe and his wife rushed to them. She hugged Sandy, and he congratulated Brad.

Brad couldn't stop grinning. His happiness knew no bounds. He wasn't even sure his feet were touching the ground.

* * *

Sandy was so surprised Brad kissed her. The unexpected move sent her heart racing, her nerves tingling, and released a fire that consumed her. A second kiss sent her emotions into the stratosphere.

Then he proposed! At first, she wasn't sure she'd heard him correctly. But he was kneeling and looking at her with pleading in his eyes. She had no choice. Her heart said *yes*, and nothing within her said *no*.

They stood on the step studying one another. He kept brushing her hair away from her face, sending flashes of electricity through her with each touch.

She didn't want this moment to end. Nor was she certain she could walk. Her insides had turned to a quivering jelly.

He pulled her to him again and wrapped her in his arms.

"Sir, we need to move on." The guide looked from Brad to the plaza and back again.

Sandy glanced out at the crowd. Almost a hundred people filled the small square. When she hopped onto the step, no one was there except Felipe and his wife.

How long have we been here? Surely not more than a few seconds. She didn't want to move out of his arms, but their time was over. She glanced up at him.

Brad nodded, and they descended the four steps to the court to additional applause. He didn't release her hand, and she made no effort to extract it. She needed the contact as an anchor. Otherwise she might float away.

* * *

They ate brisket tacos at the market, and walked, and walked, and walked. After lunch, Brad nestled Sandy's hand in his. He wanted to talk to her about their future. Wanted to make plans for the short time they would be together in Mexico and decide how to make things work once they returned to the States

Sandy was impressed with the architecture and colors of this quaint Mexican town. She was enthralled with everything she saw and reacted like she was on a drug trip. She giggled and danced. But never pulled her hand away.

He was sure she would have twirled around like the lead in a musical if he wasn't holding her hand. Her joy and enthusiasm made him happier than he'd ever been.

When the guide stopped to describe another site, he kissed her. Sometimes on the lips, sometimes on the cheek. He wanted her to know how deep his love was. Deeper than anything he'd ever experienced.

On the drive back to Queretaro, she leaned against him and rested her head on his shoulder. Within minutes she was asleep.

He closed his eyes, relishing the memory of the walk down the Kiss Alley. Something truly magical had happened on the red step. An incredible encounter with emotions beyond himself that he wanted to hold forever.

Felipe stopped at the taco shop around the corner from Aunt Molly's house. Brad wanted to celebrate and bought far too many of the delicious morsels. He was out of control. He knew it and savored every second.

Auntie M was so excited when they walked in

with the bag of treats.

While Sandy, Felipe, and his wife were busy in the kitchen getting plates and drinks, Brad sat on the couch closest to Auntie M. "Since her parents aren't here, I want to ask your permission to marry Sandy."

"You what?" The woman shook off her surprise like a dog shakes off water.

"It's simple. I've fallen in love with her, and I want to marry her." Saying the words made everything real. Since the kiss on the step, he thought he was dreaming. That this joy and happiness was just part of a movie script he was reading.

"What did Sandy say?"

"Yes." His grin sped across his face.

Auntie M patted his knee. "Then that's my answer too."

The five of them ate tacos and toasted Coca Light far into the night. Auntie M went to her bedroom about eleven. Felipe and his wife left half an hour later.

At midnight, Brad, intoxicated with delight, kissed Sandy goodnight and made it to his car.

* * *

At four o'clock Monday afternoon, Brad began his watch for the truck with red stars heading toward the science building. Since the third floor had an upgraded security system, all equipment orders for the university were being directed there. Brad checked all the invoices and arranged distribution of hundreds of boxes of supplies.

His crew had installed the lab cabinets and

countertops for an entire classroom. The stereotype of lazy workers didn't apply to these men. As they learned new skills, they were energetic and efficient.

At four-thirty, Mike Johnson called. "Mr. Andrews, I'm at the airport picking up your next order. If it's okay with you, may I deliver it tomorrow morning?"

Brad couldn't be happier agreeing to a delay.

He dismissed the crew and headed to Sandy's. He was sure Sandy and Auntie M had made lots of plans. He could hardly wait to discover what his future would look like. He could live with anything as long as Sandy was part of the scheme.

Standing at the door to their house, he rang the doorbell. No one answered. Confused he leaned against the doorframe and checked his phone. No messages.

Maybe they had gone somewhere and hadn't returned. But their car was here. Auntie M frequently called Felipe to drive them around.

He *was* earlier than normal.

Auntie M answered her phone almost as soon as it rang. "Brad, how nice for you to call."

"I haven't heard from you, so I thought I'd touch base."

The woman giggled. "Just so you know, we haven't set a date, a venue, or made a guest list. Those decisions are for you and Sandy."

Where was she? Didn't sound like a store. "I'm at your front door, and evidently you aren't home? Have I missed something?"

"You're here!" The woman screeched. "Sandy,

Brad's at the front door. Go let him in."

Through the glass door, he watched the girl of his dreams appear on the patio, dash through the house and open the door. His pulse rate jumped. She was wearing a cute translucent coverup over a two-piece bathing suit.

"I'm sorry, we were in the back yard." She did a shuffle-dance. "I'm working on my tan, and Auntie M feels better in the sun. We didn't hear the doorbell."

"I'm early."

She lowered her head and peeked at him through half-visible eyes. "I'm glad."

Did she have any idea how her teasing affected him? He stepped forward to kiss her, but she had already turned and stepped away. He chuckled. Timing was off today.

"Aunt Molly is out back. You can join her while I take a shower and get dressed." She started up the stairs.

"What if I join you instead?"

Sandy froze. She turned slowly and glared at him. "That's not a good idea. Go." She shooed him out the back door.

He laughed and stepped onto the patio.

Auntie M started to stand when he walked out the door.

"Don't get up. Sounds like we may be here a while." He collapsed into the empty lawn chair in the sun.

The woman laughed. "You're early."

"The usual four o'clock shipment is going to be delivered tomorrow morning. I sent everyone home and headed here as soon as I could get away."

"I'm sure you and Sandy have a lot to discuss."

He stood and moved his chair into shade beside Auntie M. "Tell me, do you believe in love at first sight?"

She shifted in her seat and put her elbow on the armrest. "Could be."

"I'm asking because I'm thinking about dates." *Does she want to move-in right away or wait until he heads back to the States.*

"That's going to be complicated, but I'm sure you can work it out." The woman picked up a pencil and a book of Sudoku puzzles off the TV tray beside her chair.

She glanced at Brad. "If it's God's will, everything will work out."

He stared at her. *God? What's He have to do with this?*

She turned the pages in the book. "Our plans were to go to dinner tonight, but I'm going to opt out. I think you two have a lot of talking to do and you don't need me there."

"It may be a late night…a very late night."

Auntie M tapped the pencil against an unsolved puzzle. "Are you telling me not to wait up?"

"I'm just saying…" He shrugged.

"I'm usually up most of the night anyway." She patted her sling. "Just don't make too much noise when you come in."

Chapter 10

Brad turned as Sandy stepped onto the patio. "Auntie M expects us to make all our plans by the time we come back."

His heart swelled. She wore tight white jeans and a simple pink shirt with sleeves to the elbows and buttons. She was so stunningly beautiful. Errant strands of her blonde hair, still damp from her shower, curled out of control around her face. Her skin glowed. Those robin's egg blue eyes radiated with happiness.

His gaze wandered over her body. No imperfections there either. She was even the perfect height. He was six two which would make her five five, or six or…the number didn't matter. When he hugged her, he could rest his chin on top of her head.

How lucky he was to find this California girl in the heart of Mexico. It was as if the powers that be had brought them together.

Auntie M stood, folded her chair, and leaned it against the house beside the tiny table.

Brad did the same to his lawn chair.

"Do you want us to bring you something for dinner?" Sandy led them into the house.

Auntie M laughed. "If you guys make any plans at all, it'll take a while. I'm much to hungry to wait that long. Gregory's pizza sounds great."

Sandy chuckled and smiled at Brad. "We haven't had pizza since you joined us last week."

"Well, in that case, we'll be off." He swept his hand toward the front door.

Sandy hugged her aunt, picked up her purse, and joined him in the foyer.

"You guys have a good time. And remember…" The woman sank into her recliner and popped the leg support up.

Brad guided Sandy out the door. "Remember what?"

* * *

Sandy smiled as she sat in the passenger seat while Brad held the door. "It's a family thing. Remember who you are and who your family is." *You're a child of the King.*

"That's nice. I love family traditions." He closed her door and walked around the car.

When he was settled in the driver's seat, Sandy snapped her seatbelt. "Speaking of families, tell me about yours. You've never mentioned them."

The entire drive to the restaurant Brad talked about his St. Louis clan. His hard-working dad, his overprotective mother, his younger brother and older sister.

During dinner, she told about her Northern California roots.

"So what does your dad do?" Brad sliced off another chunk of steak.

"He's a pastor."

He froze. "Like a preacher?"

Sandy laughed. "Yes."

"Oh wow. I've never dated a preacher's daughter before."

Dated? Was their special moment in Guanajuato part of some game he was playing? The declaration of love and the marriage proposal just an emotional reaction to the time and place? Good thing she discovered this before she started asking questions like *When do you want to get married?* In reality, it might not even be on his radar.

Brad touched her arm.

She turned her focus to him.

"I said, would you like to go back to my apartment, so we can work on our plans for the future."

Sandy shook her head to clear the fog of confusion that rolled in and threatened to smother her. She'd known this man for such a short period of time. Were his proclamations serious or just part of his *dating* game? "Yeah, sure. It'll be quieter there."

She was surprised when he pulled into the parking garage of the sleek tower that overlooked the city. He went to the third floor before finding a parking slot.

"You have an apartment here?" She stepped out.

"Eighth floor." He took her hand as she came

around the end of the car.

"Do you get wind sways?" She was glad she couldn't see anything but concrete columns and walls.

"What?"

She put her arm in the air and moved it back and forth. "Swaying in the wind?"

"No. It's safe." He chuckled.

Hadn't he noticed she stayed away from the ledge surrounding the plaza at the base of the Pipila monument that overlooked Guanajuato? Felipe's wife had practically hung over the ledge taking in the city view. If he hadn't picked up on hesitancy, he had no way of knowing she was afraid of heights.

Eighth floor would bother her in the middle of the city. But this building sat on the edge of a cliff. The views were probably fantastic, but... She fought panic as the elevator whirled and the floor shifted.

"Are you okay?" Brad sounded concerned.

She nodded.

He pulled her into a hug and kissed the top of her head.

She let her arms wrap around him.

The elevator doors opened, and she stepped into a hallway. Windows only ten feet away revealed the city view she was expecting. Her stomach churned, and she twirled to put her back to the windows.

They walked down a hallway that could be in any high-rise anywhere in the world. Warm tan walls and commercial carpeting in a weird design of browns, oranges and black stripes. She studied the pattern as walked to his door.

Her stomach rose to the top of her throat. Breathing became labored.

Brad opened the door. She walked into a stunning modernistic apartment decorated in gray and white with aqua and stainless-steel accents. Very professional. The curtains were drawn. No city views from eight stories above the top of a cliff.

Sandy took a deep breath. If she could quell her fears, she might find out Brad's true feelings.

"Do you have a date and place in mind?" He headed to the dark gray sofa that looked as hard as a concrete bench.

She shook her head. "What about you?" She sank onto the couch, delighted it was soft and comfortable.

"Anytime before Christmas." Before he sat down, he retrieved a pad of paper and pen from a drawer in the kitchen.

"Well that leaves lots of options." She tried to joke, but the knot in her stomach tightened.

"I can't tell you how surprised I was that you said yes to me. I expected you to slap me silly and run down the steps."

"You did?" She looked into those chocolate eyes that stole her heart the first time they met. She saw the compassion and kindness that were such a part of him. The knot loosened.

"I don't know when. I don't know how. But I do know destiny brought us together. I fell in love with you the moment you argued with Auntie M about driving back to your house. At that moment I knew I wanted to spend the rest of my life with you." He squeezed her hand then crawled his fingers up her arm to her shoulder.

His touch ignited a firestorm within her.

"I commit the rest of my life to you." His hand went behind her neck and urged her to him. She yielded.

His kiss was deep and passionate. Ripping away all restraints.

He lowered his head and kissed her neck.

New bolts of electricity sizzled through her. She ached for him.

His hand slipped inside her shirt and his fingers teased her neck. He unfastened the top button. Then the second. When he undid the fifth button, he slipped the cloth away from her chest. The tip of his finger edged inside the top of her bra.

Desires, emotions, yearnings she'd never experienced consumed her.

"I want tonight to be a night you'll always remember." He kissed where his fingers had been.

Remember! Sandy jerked back. "No, no. I can't do this." She fumbled with the buttons of her shirt.

His arm wrapped around her shoulder. He didn't say anything. Just gently, loosely held her.

After an eternity, he put his mouth just above her ear. "I love you."

Her shoulder sagged into his chest. "I love you, too. But I can't do this. Not now."

"Why not? I know you want me as much as I want you." His words were soft.

"I'm a Christian." That's all she could think to say.

"All the better. I am too." His hand ran up and

down her arm.

"Then you know that what we're thinking does not please God." She sounded like her Sunday school teacher from middle school.

"God created us with these desires. He wants us to express our love and devotion in intimate ways."

Sandy scooted away from him. It hurt worse than if she'd cut herself. "As husband and wife."

Her words seemed to stun him.

"*Only* as husband and wife." *Yes, Lord. I remember.*

He leaned back against the couch but continued to play with her hair. "I committed the remainder of my life to you."

"And I commit my life to you."

"Doesn't that make us husband and wife in God's eyes?" His hand dropped to her shoulder and a smile spread across his face.

"No. We have to make that commitment, that vow, in front of His people."

His hand flew off her shoulder. "I bet you sound just like your daddy." There was hurt in his voice.

"To honor God, I must save myself for my husband." She clasped her hands in her lap berating herself for sounding so pious.

"You're still a virgin?" He pulled away as if she had turned into a ball of fire.

She nodded.

He extended his hand as if this were a business transaction. "Nice to meet you. I haven't met a *virgin* since I left high school." He said the word with such disdain that it made her cringe.

Tears filled her eyes. "Brad, don't be like that."

Where was his compassion, his kindness?

"You're right. I'm overreacting to my disappointment. I had such great plans for us."

Had? What does that mean? Will he disappear after he drops me off? "I think you should take me home."

"Yeah, I think so."

They made their way to his vehicle without a word. Only mariachi music filled the car on the drive to Aunt Molly's. He did walk her to the door, which was a surprise. On the drive she thought he might just slow down and let her jump out.

Auntie M hadn't turned on the porch light.

He gave her a peck on the cheek.

She put her hand on his shoulder and slowly slid it down his arm. "I love you."

"You have a real funny way of showing it." He didn't move.

"I'm sorry, but I love God more."

He shook his head.

"One day, you'll understand." She was glad there was no light for him to see the tears streaming down her face.

He stepped forward. He kissed her on the lips – without the passion and desires of earlier. A kiss a big brother would plant if he had to. "I'll call tomorrow." Then he spun and left.

Sandy stood outside the door until his taillights disappeared around the corner. Had she just ended the best thing that ever happened to her? She would have to trust God for that answer.

Without a doubt, tonight was a night she would always remember.

* * *

Brad drove slowly down the street. He knew she would stand beside the door until he turned the corner. He didn't want her to think he was hurrying away. He drove two blocks before his emotions made him stop. His eyes blurred with tears and his hands shook like he was holding a jackhammer.

He didn't want to go home. He always thought the apartment felt cold. Tonight, it would be a freezer.

What had happened? He spilled out his heart to that woman and she rebuffed him. She made it sound like she was a nun or something. He was so ashamed of his reaction to her purity. And that comment about her father. He had to apologize for that as soon as possible.

If he could call her, he would. He should have bought her a phone. It was well after ten and Auntie M would most likely be asleep or numbed from drugs. He'd have to wait until tomorrow.

He should turn around, go beat on her door, and set things straight. Would she reject him again? He didn't care, he had to try. Maybe Auntie M would be on his side.

At his eighth-floor apartment, he fell onto the bed fully dressed. All night he tossed and turned. When his alarm went off at six, he wasn't sure he'd slept more than thirty minutes. If anyone else could check in the supplies and oversee the cabinetmaking, he would call in sick and go sit on Sandy's doorstep until she set a date. He would take her to buy a ring.

Instead he would replay all his mistakes from

last night as he inventoried hundreds of boxes. How exciting.

Chapter 11

Sandy awoke to the smell of bacon. She rolled over and covered her head with the pillow. What would she say to her aunt? Her best response would be *no decision.* With a groan, she forced herself out of bed and into the bathroom. She couldn't show up in the kitchen looking like she felt.

It wasn't going to take Aunt Molly long to realize something was amiss. Problem was Sandy wasn't sure *what* was wrong or if it could be fixed.

Finally, she reached the kitchen. "Good morning, Auntie M."

"I thought you were going to sleep until noon." She set a plate of bacon and over-easy eggs in front of her niece.

Last week they bought a plastic tablecloth to cover the puzzle. They reclaimed the table. This week, she needed to finish the jigsaw puzzle and bring things back to normal.

Sandy glanced at the clock. It was only nine. She picked up her fork. "I tried."

When Aunt Molly sat and put her plate of food on the table, Sandy grabbed her hand. "I'll pray." She bowed her head. *"Lord, thank you for this food to nourish our bodies. Today we need your wisdom for decisions, your encouragement, and your strength. May all we do bring honor to you. Amen."*

Auntie M gave her a questioning look before she cut her egg into little pieces.

They ate in silence.

As soon as she finished, Sandy took her dishes to the sink. It was time for her interrogation, and she dreaded this conversation.

"Well?" Her aunt tossed her napkin on her plate.

Before Sandy could respond, Auntie M's phone rang.

Brad? Sandy's stomach knotted.

Her aunt stood and moved toward the living room. "Yes, Rodger. Did you find something?"

Sandy took the plate to the sink, rinsed the dishes, and emptied the dishwasher. She loaded the dirty dishes, then wiped down all the counters. Auntie M was still chatting so Sandy swept the floor and took out the garbage. As she walked back into the living room Aunt Molly was still talking. Sandy glanced at the notebook in her aunt's lap. It was filled with writing.

Auntie M waved for Sandy to sit on the couch.

"Yes. That will be great. If I run into problems, I'll call you…soon."

She paused and put more notes on her page.

"Okay, we'll see you then." She turned to

Sandy. "Plans have changed." Her voice quivered. "Rodger sees what is causing my pain. I have broken and twisted bones in my wrist and the bones in the arm aren't lined up right. Good news, he can do something about it."

"That's wonderful!" Sandy clapped.

"And he wants to do it right away. I'm healing incorrectly and the sooner he fixes it the better." As she talked she was punching the computer keyboard. "Oh, what a blessing. I can do it!"

Sandy watched her aunt and waited. A million questions flew through her mind.

Aunt Molly made a phone call and spoke in rapid Spanish. "*Excelente. Gracias.*" Then, more Spanish. Tears streamed down her face.

When had her aunt learned to speak Spanish like that? Had she been coy with Brad when he spoke in Spanish to others around them. *You are a sly one, Auntie M.*

What's happening? From her aunt's expression, whatever the news was, it was good. Sandy relaxed.

Auntie M disconnected and held the phone in a death grip in her lap. She leaned her head back and closed her eyes. "God is good. Only He could do this."

Sandy wanted to scream. Her stomach suddenly convulsed.

"When Brad comes over tonight, we're going to have a lot to talk about." Auntie M hadn't moved.

"What's going on?" Sandy's voice was louder than she intended.

Her aunt's hand flew into the air to tell her to wait. After a few seconds, she opened her eyes and smiled at Sandy. "I'm sorry, I just had to offer a quick prayer of thanksgiving. Rodger, my friend in Dallas has found why my arm's hurting. He wants to do surgery. I've made reservations for both of us to get to Dallas."

Sandy studied her aunt. Last week she said she wanted to move back to the States if something could be done for her arm.

"The packers will come tomorrow and pick up my stuff Thursday. Our flight on Friday is at nine in the morning. We'll get to Dallas about eleven-thirty. I need to be at the hospital in Dallas by four so they can do some pre-surgery tests."

The flood of information assaulted Sandy's senses. Today was Tuesday. How could she get all this scheduled? "You did all that? I thought things in Mexico moved slower. What you're saying is fast...very fast." *No, no. Not without Brad.*

"Actually, I had decided before you came to move back to the States. It was just a matter of when. I had talked to the movers about possibilities and set up an account. Last week I called again and set tentative dates for the packers to come tomorrow. I was hoping Rodger could do something and I wanted to be prepared. God is blessing and working things out."

"Auntie M you continually amaze me." Quivers ran through Sandy's body. In three days, she would be leaving Mexico and Brad. Could they get things settled before she left?

The rest of the day, Sandy helped Auntie M pack the things she would need for a couple of months. Her belongings would be shipped to

Arizona. Once medical issues were resolved, Sandy needed to find a job. Then, and only then, could they find a house for Auntie M.

All day Sandy's thoughts turned to Brad. She anxiously awaited his arrival for dinner. At five, she heard her aunt's phone. A few minutes later the woman came up the stairs.

"Brad can't come tonight. My phone was in the kitchen, and I didn't get to it before he left a voice message. He got two truckloads of materials at four and has to inventory them before he can leave."

Sandy thought she would cry. Disappointment hurt. What if something happened tomorrow, and she couldn't see him? They were going to a hotel Thursday and to Dallas on Friday. From her packing days, they would go to a hotel as soon as the packers finished.

So many changes, so much happening. And Brad was at work and didn't know. She should have told him about the possibilities of them returning to the States when Auntie M talked about it. But no, she had to wait until all their plans were made. Now their departure was imminent, and he didn't know.

She tried to call him twice, but they went straight to voicemail. The second time she left a message. "Brad, some things have happened here, and I need to talk to you as soon as possible. No one's hurt, but …please call soon."

Was this God's way saying Brad wasn't *The One*?

* * *

After calling Auntie M, Brad's energy drained from him like the run-off from a summer rainstorm.

He could have handled one truckload of goods, but not two.

The afternoon shipment included the chemical cabinets he'd been waiting for. As soon as those were installed, he could fill them with the boxes of test tubes, flasks, and other scientific equipment needed for learning and research. And the third-floor storage rooms would become laboratories.

The project was coming together.

Which meant, his time in Mexico was limited.

If he could get the boxes secured before eight, he would go see Sandy. He had never been so trapped by work. It wouldn't be so bad if things hadn't ended so terribly Monday.

He'd called twice but the calls went to voicemail. He couldn't say to Auntie M the things he wanted to say to Sandy. Finally, he told her he wouldn't be over for dinner. How he hated those words.

Brad left campus at midnight.

Wednesday morning on his way back to school, he dialed Auntie M.

Nothing.

He looked at his phone while at a stoplight. *Dead*! He hadn't plugged it into the charger last night. Frustration bubbled up in him. He hit the steering wheel with the palm of his hand. Thankfully, he had a charger in his desk.

When he arrived at his office, another shipment of boxes was waiting to be unloaded. It's unusual to get early morning shipments here. If they had been in America, these would be arriving in eighteen wheelers, not large vans. He would have been overwhelmed once, and not this constant pressure.

Somehow, he had survived twenty-four hours without seeing or hearing from his blonde damsel-in-distress. He wasn't sure he could do that for the next twenty-four. He wanted her by his side. They would be talking about living together if it weren't for her religious hang-ups.

He'd never understood how someone could believe in something they couldn't see or touch. He snickered. He'd told Sandy he was a Christian. He didn't even know what that meant, but it sounded good at the time. Her beliefs were important to her. He needed to check out her religion. He didn't want it to become a bigger problem than it already was.

About noontime, he pulled out his phone to call Sandy. He was determined to talk to her. To tell her he was sorry and wanted to make amends. *Dead*! He'd hurried to the loading dock when he arrived this morning and never charged the phone.

He ran to his office and plugged in the charger. He had missed Sandy's call. Her voice sounded empty and sad. Something was going on at Auntie M's. Her plea rang in his ears. *Please call.* And he hadn't.

He punched Auntie M's icon. His call went straight to voicemail. That was odd. "Hey guys, my phone went dead, and I haven't been able to call. It's on the charger now, so I'll talk to you soon. See you tonight."

Later on his way to their house, he realized he'd left his phone on the charger. When he arrived, the lights were off, and the car gone.

Another blunder. Had they left a message, and

he didn't get it?

He waited an hour before he crept home. How could he have missed her? Where were she and Auntie M? Could he enjoy life without Sandy by his side?

Thursday, he left campus at noon. He'd tried to call Sandy twice, but the call went to voicemail.

Today, he would convince Sandy of his deep love for her.

He pulled into the *privada* at one o'clock. His heart raced as he rehearsed his declaration of apology and love. By the time he approached her house, he was shaking with anticipation.

Their car wasn't in the carport.

He hopped out of his vehicle and raced to the front door. No one answered.

He glanced through the glass door. Something was different inside. Auntie M's pictures weren't on the wall. Her knick-knacks weren't on the buffet. What had happened? He collapsed onto the doorframe. He turned and looked inside the house again. His stomach convulsed.

"You looking for Miss Molly?" A gardener stood on the sidewalk with his rake in his hand.

"Yes, do you know where she is?" Brad stepped off the porch and approached him.

"No. She moved this morning. Don't know where she went."

"Moved?" An intense burning started in Brad's neck and descended to his toes.

"Yes. Miss Molly going to hospital. She not come back." The man seemed pleased he could pass on this information in English.

"Her furniture is here." Brad waved his hand toward the front door. His disbelief dominated his thinking.

"No, no. Chairs with house."

A furnished rental.

Brad sank onto the ledge along the sidewalk. "She's gone?"

"Her and the young one. They go."

Brad called Auntie M's phone, but it went to voicemail. "I'm at your house, and the gardener said you moved. Where are you? What's happened? Please call soon. Sandy, I love you. I'll come to you as soon as I can."

When he called again at suppertime, the phone had been disconnected.

Brad ate dinner alone at the taco shop around the corner from Auntie M's house.

Chapter 12

Sandy picked up the garment bag with the Mary costume inside. The heaviness she'd carried since their sudden departure from Mexico hadn't lessened. She hoped all the decorating and activities around Christmas would distract her from her emptiness. It hadn't worked.

"Are you ready?" Auntie M bounced into the room.

Sandy laughed. "I think you're more excited about this program than I am."

Her aunt swung her arms out. "You're a star. The lead female role in the Dallas Holiday Musical is a major accomplishment."

"You do remember the gal who had that role moved to Las Vegas, and I'm filling in because I'm the youngest in the choir." She hugged the bag.

"Don't be silly." Auntie M plopped on the bed.

"The director actually said that the role was given to me because he didn't think a fifty-year-old made a good Mary." She glanced at her watch.

"How old is Joseph?" Her aunt smoothed the bedspread when she rose.

Sandy stepped toward the door. "I have no idea. Doc hasn't been at a rehearsal since I started. He's been on a mission trip. Over in Africa, I think."

"Why would they give him the role? Has he been doing it for years?" Aunt Molly followed.

"Evidently he has the most quote luscious unquote baritone voice I've ever heard. Tonight, I'll find out."

"Let's hope so."

"Doc's a new Christian who's really on fire for the Lord. Last spring, he had a major trauma in his life and as a result, he sought out God. Since then, he turned down a high paying job in the private sector and became a specialist missionary. Whatever that is. I'll talk with him tonight and find out."

Her aunt wobbled her head from side to side. "Maybe. Just maybe he can heal your heart."

I don't want my heart healed. I committed my life to Christ and to Brad. I just have to adjust better. But don't crimp her dreams. "No one knows what the future brings."

"That's the truth." Aunt Molly patted her arm. "Just look what one comment from Ellen did. Within a couple of weeks, my arm was healed. Now it's good as new."

"You got your miracle." Sandy smiled and picked up her purse. "What time are Mom and Dad arriving tomorrow?"

"About noon. They wanted to be sure they got

here for your opening."

Sandy smiled. While waiting for Auntie M to come out of surgery last spring, she had spent the time in the chapel talking to God. She told God that until He interceded, she would honor her vow to Brad. Her peace was unbelievable.

Moving to Frisco was a blessing to everyone. Auntie M's arm healed. Sandy landed a fabulous job, and they found the perfect house for her aunt's retirement. If Sandy didn't have a hole in her heart, all would be perfect.

As she walked into the auditorium, Sandy's nerves spiked. What was she doing? She'd never sung the lead in a musical before. She'd never even been *in* a musical before. Church choirs were the limit of her experience. She had practiced and knew what to do. She would come on stage carrying the baby Jesus, a Cabbage Patch doll, and sit on the bale of hay. She was to hold the baby until Joseph began. Then, she would put the baby into the manger and turn to face the man with the luscious baritone voice everyone talked about.

Her solo focused on establishing that Jesus provided a way for man to come into the presence of God without hesitation. Joseph's song was about receiving God's love and sharing it with the world. The man who would sing that role was doing that with his life. He arrived back from a mission trip late last night. What a perfect role-cast.

The dress rehearsal proceeded without a flaw. As the time for her song approached, the knot in her stomach tightened. What was it her father always said *do it to honor God.* She said a quick prayer, picked up the Cabbage Patch Jesus, and entered right on cue. As she sat down on the scratchy bale, a commotion in the background surprised her. But she managed to continue to the end of the song right on beat.

What's a dress rehearsal without at least one miscue?

The interlude for Joseph's song began.

Sandy was so eager to hear this voice.

He began, but he sang the wrong words. Instead of 'God's love for you is never ending,' he said 'my love for you is never ending'. The voice short-circuited her brain. The baritone was the same rich sound that asked her if he could help at the check-out counter in Mexico. *Brad*? No, that had to be her imagination. This man's name was Doc. By the second phrase, she jumped to her feet.

The baby doll rolled across the floor as she turned to face Doc.

She beheld Brad's face as he mouthed the words *I love you.*

His arms spread welcoming her into a hug. She ran to him. At their embrace, the orchestra stopped playing. When he kissed her, the choir applauded.

"Brad, oh Brad!" Tears streamed down her cheeks and onto his shoulder.

"Sandy, I thought I'd lost you" He held her tighter.

"Me, too." She stretched up and kissed him.

"Five-minute break," the director yelled.

Brad took her hand and raced up the aisle to the lobby. He twirled her around and pulled her close.

While in a hug, tears streamed down Sandy's face. "Auntie M had disconnected her phone before they got in touch with him. We thought we'd reach you during the day or at least in the evening. They cut the phone off about five. Auntie M told me as soon as we got to the States on Friday, we'd get new phones and transfer the contacts."

Brad wiped her tears with his thumb.

"Did you know contacts will transfer but recent calls don't? Auntie M never added you to her contact list." She laid her head against his chest. "I tried for over a week to find you. I even called The University of Arkansas to track you down. They didn't even know you existed."

Brad laughed. "You'd have had better luck if you called Arkansas State University."

Sandy giggled into his chest.

He loosened the hug. "I'm sorry. I said a bunch of stuff I shouldn't have, and I wanted to do things that were out of line. Will you ever forgive me? I was such a jerk. I told you I was a Christian, but I wasn't. I wanted you to…"

She nodded.

She touched his lips with her finger. "Oh, Brad. So many mistakes. So much lost time." Tears sprang to her eyes.

"Shhh, shhh." He brushed her hair back from her face. "You took a stand for God. I'd never known anyone to stand up for their beliefs like that. I wanted to find out why. I contacted a friend who introduced me to his pastor. That man led me to Jesus. I found forgiveness. I found God. And now, I've found you, again."

"You are my lost hero, and now found."

He kissed her. "How's Auntie M's arm?"

"Completely healed, good as new." She turned her head as the orchestra began playing.

"Before we go back." He stepped away from her but continued to hold her hand. "Do remember in Mexico you asked me when I wanted to get married?"

"And you said, before Christmas."

He pulled her into a tight embrace. "We still have time."

Dress rehearsal proceeded without incident.

Sandy remembered little after they reentered the auditorium. Brad introduced her as the girl he lost in Mexico, but God brought back to him. She sang the songs as best she could with this man's presence distracting her.

As they left the stage, the director stopped them. "Congratulations. But Doc, I want you to know, tomorrow night, no pauses." He laughed as he walked away.

"Doc. Where did that name come from?" Sandy led the way to the dressing area.

"I completed my doctorate. The guy that introduced me to this group always called me Doc. It just stuck."

"Sorry, mister. You're Brad."

He pulled her away from the door. "I'm going to follow you home. Hurry and change."

As they drove up the Dallas North Tollway, she slowed. No way did she want to lose this guy in traffic. They had already exchanged phone numbers and laughed as they put them into their contact lists. In case they got separated.

As they walked into the house, Sandy could hardly contain her excitement. "Auntie M, I brought someone home."

"That's nice, dear. Who is it?" Her voice came from the living room.

Sandy gazed into Brad's gleaming eyes. She wrapped her arm around his waist. "My hero."

Epilogue

On Christmas Eve, Sandy stood in the foyer of the chapel in her church with Auntie M. The sanctuary was decorated with candles and silver ribbons and looked like a wonderland. The perfect background for a fairytale wedding.

"It's so pretty." Auntie M stretched up to peek through the window in the back door of the sanctuary.

"It's Brad's doing. He took the decorations for tonight's midnight service and added to it. I don't know how he knew that I'd love them, but he insisted on adding those silver bows to the candleholders and the large ones to the pews. It's magical how they reflect the lights from the electric candles."

"Electric?" Auntie M stared through the pane.

"Fire codes don't allow for flaming candles." Sandy shifted her weight from one foot to another. "They look real, don't they?"

Brad's brother, their only usher, had just sat his parents.

Her mom dashed down the hall to be next to enter. She gave Sandy a quick kiss. "I'm so happy for you." She turned and headed to her seat.

"Your mom is half-way down the aisle. Isn't it wonderful both your parents stayed in town after the musical?" Her aunt relaxed and leaned against the doorframe.

"I heard her and Mrs. Andrews saying how concerned they were because Brand and I had such heavy hearts. And now, I'm having trouble keeping mine in my chest. Aunt Molly, I've never been happier."

"Or looked prettier." The older woman smoothed the skirt of Sandy's dress.

Sandy fidgeted with the lace overlay. She loved the sweetheart neckline and long flared skirt.

Her father came down the hall carrying two bouquets. "Oh, Sandy. You are so beautiful. My little girl is all grown up."

Sandy's face heated.

He handed his sister her flowers and kissed her. "Thank you for all you've done for Sandy."

Auntie M blushed. Sandy smiled. It's the first time Sandy's seen the woman's cheeks redden.

The sanctuary doors opened. Brad, his father, and the pastor entered from the side of the altar.

After a pause, organ music began.

Her adorable aunt walked down the aisle. Sandy giggled as she gave Brad an okay sign. The small gathering chuckled.

Mendelssohn's Wedding March began, and she

stepped forward with her dad. Brad turned and smiled. He waited for her.

Her heart soared. She drew a deep breath and walked slowly in cadence with the music, but she wanted to run into his arms. Last spring, she lost her hero, and now he was found. As she approached this man of her dreams she kept squeezing her hand to be sure all this was real. Soon she and Brad would join their lives for eternity. She'd never lose him again.

Kathy Wall graduated from Bradley University in Peoria, IL, with a degree in elementary education. She taught school then took a sabbatical to raise two children. Her husband's job resulted in many, many moves (she stopped counting at 25.) She put my teaching career on hold and began freelance writing. She did local newspaper stories and branched out into travel articles – all non-fiction. When they settled in the Dallas area, she returned to teaching. She and her husband were foster parents for seven years.

While in Indianapolis in the late 1990's, Kathy began quilting. The interest became a passion and you will find references to quilting in many of her books.

After retirement, she returned to writing, but focused on fiction. With the teaching and encouragement of ACFW and Lena Nelson Dooley, her life changed. She currently attends a weekly critique group for writing, a quilt group for sewing, and her church for inspiration and guidance.

List of all published books

Never Again
Trust Wyatt No!

Someone Special
The Gift Quilt

Made in the USA
Columbia, SC
17 March 2020